# When An Amish Heart Breaks

Marisa Meyer

Published by Trellis Publishing, 2021.

This is a work of fiction. Similarities to real people, places, or events are entirely coincidental.

WHEN AN AMISH HEART BREAKS

**First edition. July 11, 2021.**

Copyright © 2021 Marisa Meyer.

ISBN: 979-8224597543

Written by Marisa Meyer.

# WHEN AN AMISH HEART BREAKS

## MARISA MEYER

# Chapter 1

The wind howled through the treetops and the rain sleeted against Rachel's face as she ran blindly into the darkness, soaked and cold, but desperate to get away. Away from the pain away from the life she knew. How could they simply put her mamm in the ground and expect her to continue with life? Sobs tore through her chest as she stumbled through the darkness. Her mamm wasn't supposed to die, not yet.

She was only sixteen, her mamm was supposed to be there for when she turned eighteen, and when she got married, but instead, Gott had taken her away. The pain of losing her mother had left Rachel fragile. Gott had forsaken her and with that her hope was lost.

Her mamm had been her compass all these years, teaching her and guiding her in the ways of Herr Gott.

She had finally made it to the main road, and with her arms wrapped around her she walked in the direction of the city. She had to get to Mary.

Mary, her best friend, had left on Rumspringa over a year ago, and had written her letters. She had told her how wonderful life was with the Englischers and how many friends she had made. When Mary first came to tell her she was leaving, Rachel had been shocked. Mary had been the last person, she thought, who would want to leave. Yet, she did, with the promise to one day return, but a year later, Mary had met a young man who she had fallen in love with.

Rachel walked and walked and her mind was a chaotic mess as she tried to make sense of it all. As she came over the rise of the hill, lights illuminated the road and her shadow extended ahead of her. Nervous, she picked up her pace. Having been cocooned in a life away from the dangers of modern society, anxiety set in. What is she had made a mistake?

The automobile drew closer and through the pelting rain and wind she could hear the quiet hum of the motor as it slowed down.

A yellow car pulled up and the driver wound down the window. "Do you need a ride somewhere?"

It was a young woman, and her anxiety eased somewhat.

"No, I'm fine," she said as she continued walking.

The woman rolled on next to her, "Come on, it's raining and you're soaked. I can give you a ride to the next town."

Rachel hesitated as she looked up ahead, but she could only see a few feet ahead of her. With the rain curtaining the distance from her view, she had no idea how far it was to the next town. This may be her only chance to get that far. She glanced over at the woman, whose eyes peaked at her through the narrow open window.

"Come along," the woman said, "You're going to get sick out in the rain."

With a slight nod, Rachel hurried around the back of the car and got into the passenger seat.

The woman reached in the back seat and pulled out a small blanket. "Here, put this over your wet clothes before you catch a cold."

"Denki," she whispered and wrapped the blanket around her shoulders.

"So where you headed?"

Rachel looked out the window, "I'm going to my friend."

"Right and where's that?"

"Muncie," Rachel whispered.

"Wow, you were going to walk there?" the woman blurted and then quickly smiled, "The name's Joanna by the way."

"I'm Rachel."

Silence fell between the two of them for a brief moment before Joanna spoke again. "So, I gather from your clothes, you're Amish?"

Rachel hugged the blanket tighter around her shoulders, "Jah."

"Not one for many words I see."

"I'm sorry, but how far is it to the next town?"

Rachel turned on the demister in the car, and edged forward to see through the window, "I'm actually on my way to Anderson, so I'm happy to drop you in Muncie on my way."

"Oh no, I-I- you can just drop me at the next town," Rachel objected.

Joanna laughed, "Oh nonsense, I'm going in that direction, anyway. Do you have your friend's address?"

Realisation swept over Rachel, she had Mary's address in her apron pocket, and with her clothes soaked it may be ruined. In a slight panic she dug in the pocket to retrieve the small folded up envelope and relief washed over her. The address was still visible on the back of the envelope.

"Here," she whispered, "This is where Mary lives."

"Hang on to that, it's another hour before we get there. We'll stop up ahead at the gas station. I have some dry clothes for you."

A while later Rachel stood in front of the faded, cracked mirror in the restroom looking at her reflection. Joanna had given her a set of dry clothes, and the person looking back at her looked like a complete stranger.

Dressed in jeans and a t-shirt, with a baseball cap instead of her prayer kapp, she felt guilty. All her life she had lived a life dedicated to the church and their religion, but here she was, disobedient and rebellious.

She worried her bottom lip and turned sideways.

"Eh, Rachel, are you coming?" Joanne called from outside, "We need to make tracks."

Rachel pursed her lips and determined she took her wet clothes and dumped it into the waste bin. She owned Gott nothing, not a single thing. This was her time to go out and start a new life. It was His fault, her mamm died.

She stepped out of the restroom and Joanna gasped in mocked surprise, "Just look at you, you will fit right in!"

An hour later, they arrived in Muncie and Joanne took her to the Mary's place. This was the last time she would ever see the kind Englisch woman, but she would never forget her.

# Chapter 2

Rachel had never been in a modern house; Mary even had a television and a radio. Feeling somewhat out of place, she remained seated on the sofa, studying her surroundings.

"I still can't believe you're here," Mary said and put a cup of hot chocolate in front of her on the coffee table.

"I had to get away; I couldn't stand being home anymore."

Mary sat down opposite her, "I can imagine. It must have been a tough choice."

Rachel nodded, "Not as tough as I would have thought. After *mamm's* funeral and the way Bishop Fischer made it sound like she no longer mattered, I couldn't cope. I-I..." her bottom lip trembled, "I just wish they had allowed her to go to the *dokter*."

Mary sighed and took a sip of her hot chocolate, "That is exactly why I couldn't stay there. I miss some things, but their primitive way of thinking, and failure to embrace the modern world and what it had to offer, was a big wake-up call."

Rachel lowered her eyes. Her mamm had warned her against the technologies of the modern Englisch world and the evils they bring into the homes. "I guess in some way, it keeps the evil of this world out of our homes..."

"Utter nonsense," huffed Mary, "I've had TV and a radio, I even have a cell phone, and I don't think my soul is lost because of it. There is a lot of churches here in the city, they all believe the bible, but they don't condemn you over every little thing."

"For certain?" Rachel asked curiously.

"I'm telling you, and here, parents accept their children regardless of the choices they make. They don't shun you based on your life choices, they embrace it."

Rachel's heart ached for her friend; the bitterness in her tone was clear. Mary hadn't seen her parents ever since she left and her *daett* had refused to have any further contact with her. Although, occasionally she received a letter from her *mamm*, she knew she could never go back. Once shunned, always shunned, and this would be Rachel's future.

Over the next two days, Rachel tried to fit in as best she could. Mary had given her a few outfits to help with her transformation and promised to help her settle in. Thanks to her mother, she had enough money to get by for a few weeks before she would have to make a plan and earn a living. But as daunting as it was, she would do whatever it takes.

"Rachel, meet Stephen," Mary introduced, "Stephen, this is my friend Rachel. The one I told you about?"

The young man stood with his hands tucked in his pants pockets; pants that fit him like a second skin. His hair was short and spiky and the first thing Rachel noticed was the tattoo of a serpent on his forearm.

"Hallo," she said with feigned composure. "It's a pleasure to meet you."

He looked her up and down and nodded, "So how long are you planning on staying?"

Rachel's eyes shot to Mary's, and she sucked in her bottom lip, "Just for a few days."

"Rachel will stay here until she is settled, why do you always have to be so rude?"

Mary hooked her arm into Rachel's and dragged her to the door, "I'm taking her out to buy some clothes, go stay with your friends for a while."

"I just got here."

"And now you're leaving."

Stephen mumbled something unmentionable under his breath and Rachel stood frozen. She really hoped for the sake of her soul, she wouldn't have to meet people like him.

By the end of the week, it had gone smoother than what she expected. After a few days, experiencing a world she had been shielded from her entire life, Rachel was ready to settle in and embrace it. There was no turning back now, no mother, not father and no family back home.

On her knees next to her bed she sat, unable to utter a single word. Guilt had weaved its way into her soul and knowing she had deliberately turned her back on her faith prevented her from praying. But somehow, kneeling in the stillness that surrounded her brought her some peace.

# Chapter 3

It has been a week since Rachel's disappearance, and Michael was getting more worried by the day. He knew where she was. Several weeks before her mother died, she had told him how much she wanted to venture out into the world and find her friend Mary. It was the only logical explanation, and after what his dad had said to her at the funeral, he knew in his mind she had gone to her old friend.

With his bible resting on his lap, and the dim glow of the lantern casting a comforting ambiance around his small room, he closed his eyes and prayed. He had been friends with Rachel since they were kinner, and leaving her to make a bad choice, because of something someone had said was as good as handing her a knife to take her own life. And he could never live with himself, knowing he hadn't tried to help her.

"Michael!" yelled his *daett*, "Don't you dare walk away from me boy!"

He gritted his teeth and balled his fists, then slowly turned to face his *daett*, "I will be back soon, I promise."

"**Nein**! I will not let you run a fool's errand after a girl."

He stood and looked from his mamm to his *daett*, searching their expressions. He could see his *mamm* was on his side, but she wouldn't dare go against his word.

"*Daett*, I can't let Rachel throw her soul away to the dogs."

"*Dat* is her choice, she ran away of her own free will, you are no saviour! If you leave, you may as well stay away," his *daett* muttered.

Shocked and angered, Michael took a deep steadying breath, "Is it not the Herr Gott, who says, I will feed My flock, and I will lead them to rest. I will seek the lost, bring back the scattered and bind up the broken?" He walked over to where his mamm stood with her hand covering her mouth. "Mamm, I will come back, but I cannot let Rachel go astray less I try to convince her where her home is."

"Joseph, let the boy go," his mamm said. "He's doing what Herr Gott would want."

"*Denki* mamm," he whispered and hugged her. His *daett* was silent.

Michael, holding a small piece of paper in one hand and a suitcase in the other, walked the streets of Muncie. Street names unfamiliar to him, but he had some sense of direction. When he finally found Grove Avenue, relieve washed over him. He could only hope she was here. He had taken a wild guess when he left home to find her, but something deep down spurred him on, and as he walked down the street, looking at the house numbers, his heart raced.

"Who is it?" Rachel called from behind the closed door.

Mary had gone to work, and usually her friends wouldn't come over until she was home. There was another knock and Rachel reached for the door knob, "Mary isn't here," she tried again.

"Rachel? Is that you?"

Her heart thudded in her chest. The voice sounded very familiar. "Michael?" she asked nervously.

"Rachel, yes, it's me Michael."

She gripped the door knob and pressed her forehead against the door. She never, for a moment, expected anyone to come and find her, yet, here he was. About to open the door she paused. She was dressed in modern clothing and she wasn't wearing her *kapp*. What if Michael judges her?

"You shouldn't have come," she said from behind closed doors.

"Well I am here am I not? Open the door."

She worried her bottom lip. He had come all this way, and for her to send him away without offering him food, would be rude. Nervously she turned the door knob, and the door clicked open.

Michael had no idea what to expect when he heard her voice on the other side of the door, but what he saw had left him speechless. Dressed in a floral-print dress with short sleeves and her blonde hair flowing freely over her shoulders, she didn't look at all like the Rachel he had known.

"Rachel…" he breathed, "I was worried about you."

A frown drew her brows together, "How did you know where to find me?"

He smiled and took out the small piece of paper. "You told me you wanted to find Mary."

"You thought I was foolish."

"I did, but I also did not expect things to take the turn it did."

She rolled her eyes, and he shifted his weight, "Can I come in?"

Stepping aside she let him in and he glanced around the house. "So this is where you have been staying?"

"Why are you here Michael?"

"I came to bring you back home."

He would not lie and pretend he came for a visit, he made his intentions clear. She belonged back home where he could take care of her. When she didn't respond he turned and met her gaze and saw nothing but resentment in those sky blue eyes.

"Rachel, I understand how angry you must have been. But my *daett* had only meant good. We all loved your *mudder, verschteh*?"

"*Nein*, I do not understand. I do not understand why the church prevented my mamm from getting the medical help she needed. While she suffered day in and day out, no one bothered to see beyond the *Ordnung* and the stupid rules."

He could relate to her anger, he too had been there. Aged twenty-three, he too had lost some close friends and relatives. But he trusted and believed Herr Gott had the power over life and death, and if Gott's plan included death, who was he to question it.

"I know how you feel, remember when my *grossmammi* died? I was also angry. I also believed if she got the right help, she could survive, but what did you tell me?"

Rachel spun around and walked further into the house and he went after her.

"What was it you told me? Let Gott's will prevail?"

The last thing he wanted to do was chase her further away, but she had to hear the truth. He reached out for her and grabbed her by the arm. "Don't run away Rachel," he whispered. "You know in your heart, this is not the path Gott has chosen for you."

Her eyes shimmered with tears as she looked at him and Michael's heart ached for her. Out of sight, it was so easy to pull her into his arms and hold her until her shoulders stopped shaking and her sobs grew silent.

"Please come home," he said against her hair, before stepping away from her and searching her eyes.

"This is my home now," she mumbled. "I have nothing to go home to."

His stomach twisted. Was she so bitter, she didn't think of him as a friend anymore? Jah, of course his *daett* had spurred her into running away, but he wasn't like his *daett*. He cared for her, he had since forever. Even when they were just kinner, he knew Rachel would be the woman he would marry one day. But he knew better than to push her.

"All right, if you plan on making this your home, I will have to do the same."

Her brows shot up, and she looked at him in shock, "You're being a *dummkopp*! You can't just stay here."

"Of course I can. I am not leaving here without you."

Rachel huffed, threw her hands in the air and stormed to her room, leaving Michael stranded in the living room.

# Chapter 4

Early, one Sunday morning, three days after Michael's arrival, Rachel busied herself by making breakfast. Ignoring him had been a complete failure, and Mary wasn't helping either. For some reason beyond her comprehension, Mary had almost been excited to see him.

Usually Mary would make breakfast, since Rachel had no idea how to operate the modern appliances, but today, she would make it work.

She had seen her friend use the toasting machine to toast the pre-sliced bread, and she also noted how to use the coffee maker. How hard could it possibly be?

"She's hurting," she heard Mary whisper, while she popped two slices of bread into the toaster.

"You think I don't know that?" Michael said, "But you know as well, she doesn't belong here in the city."

It was hard for her not to listen to their conversation; after all, they were discussing her future.

"Look," Mary whispered, "As much as I want to agree with you, it's her choice, the only problem is, I can't... well, I can't really afford to have her stay here for much longer. Stephen is already irate, because he has to sleep at his friend's place."

"Who is Stephen?"

Caught up in the conversation, Rachel scooted closer to the door to hear better and tossed the tea towel on the counter.

"It's my boyfriend," she heard Mary whisper.

"You stay with him?" Michael said condescendingly.

With her back up against the wall and out of sight, she held her breath not wanting them to notice her. But it was obvious that she was only in the way. Her selfishness had brought her to a place, where she didn't fit in, and where she wasn't really wanted.

"What's that smell?" Mary asked.

"Something is burning," said Michael.

Rachel looked up and saw the flames licking the bottom of the overhead cupboards above the toasting machine. In error, she had tossed the tea towel without paying attention, and it had caught alight.

"Oh no!" she cried and rushed over to the flames, and with her bare hands she slapped at the fire, trying to put it out. With no regard for her own safety, and the heat of the flames stinging her hands, she desperately tried.

"Rachel! What are you doing?"

In a panic she grabbed the jug filled with water and aimed for the fire, but in a blink of an eye, strong arms were wrapped around her upper body and the jug went crashing to the floor. A loud blowing sound tore through the kitchen and then everything was shrouded in a white cloud.

A while later, while Mary was busy on the phone trying to get a hold of Stephen, and Rachel sat in the bedroom with Michael opposite her.

"I know what you're thinking," she muttered.

"You cannot know a thing I'm thinking Rachel," he said without looking at her.

With her left hand laying open on her lap, Michael lifted her other hand and carefully inspected the burns. "Fsst..." she hissed as the pain radiated from her palm into her arm.

"Sorry," Michael apologized as he gently applied the Aloe Vera gel Mary had given him.

Rachel struggled to hold still, every time Michael tried to touch her hand, or apply the gauze it stung like a thousand bees. But somehow it also brought her some relief that he was here to tend to her wounds.

"We must keep an eye on your burns," he murmured as he took her other hand, "This one wasn't as badly burnt. What were you thinking?"

Rachel closed her eyes and lowered her head, "I wasn't thinking. I saw the fire, and I panicked."

"You're such a *dummkopp*," he said, but she could hear the smile in his voice. "How would you ever learn to cope in a modern world like this?"

She opened her eyes and met his gaze and became aware of his thumb grazing the inside of her wrist. Her breath hitched slightly, and she pulled her hand away. "How did you learn to make honey without getting stung a few times?" she countered.

"Rachel, it's not the same as making honey, this is changing your entire life and everything you once believed in. Your mamm would turn over in her grave, knowing you had run off to the city."

Tears sprung to her eyes, and she rose to her feet. "Who cares what my mamm would think? She's dead now."

"If not for your mamm, think of me. I've known you since we were young," he said as he came to stand behind her, resting his hands on her shoulders. The warmth and tenderness of his touch spread through her body like wild fire.

An awkward silence passed between them and Rachel held her breath. What was he implying, and why was he talking as if there was some sort of future for them? His *daett* would never approve of any such a notion.

A soft knock on the door drew their attention, and she quickly stepped out of Michael's reach.

"Sorry to interrupt," Mary said, "I um..." she hesitated, "Well, Stephen is on his way home, but he's not too happy about the whole incident," she swallowed. "Rachel, you know I would love to help you, but I have my own life here now. You can't stay here anymore."

Rachel felt numb. The one friend she thought, who would have helped her, has turned her away. And now she had nowhere to go. Dejected, she glanced at her friend, and then at Michael. "I understand," she murmured, fighting back the tears.

"I've booked a motel room for you, I mean it aint much, but it's a roof over your head for a few days while you figure things out."

Her friend looked genuinely troubled and conflicted, but she had her own life, and Rachel knew, she had no right to expect anything more than what Mary had offered.

An hour later, Rachel stood hugging her friend Mary. "I will be forever grateful for you," she mumbled through the tears.

"I'm just a phone call away, whatever you decide to do, I'll be here to listen," Mary said.

"I know. Take care of yourself."

"And you too."

A yellow taxi cab pulled up and Michael held the door open for her.

Like every person she cared for and loved, Mary too, was gone, and there was nothing she could do to change that.

## Chapter 5

"Are you awake?" Rachel asked later that evening.

"Mhm. *Vas itz letz?*"

At first, when they arrived at the motel, Rachel had been shocked to discover there was only one room, with one bed. And realizing she would have to share the room with Michael was almost too much. But he had agreed to take the floor while she takes the bed.

"Why did you really come to Muncie?" she said, breaking the silence.

She could hear him shuffle on the floor as he moved, and she held her breath, but he didn't appear next to her.

"I told you, I came to bring you back."

She stared up at the mouldy patch on the ceiling and worried her lip. "What if I don't want to go back?"

"Then I must stick around a while longer."

A smile spread on her lips and she held her breath. Michael had always been there for her, but she never considered him to be anything more than a dear friend. But his actions spoke louder than words. The fact that he had made an effort to find her after she had run away from home, said more than enough.

"Rachel?" she heard him say. "Are you awake?"

"Jah," she said softly.

"Why didn't you come to me when you were hurting?"

She turned on to her side and tucked her hands under her cheek, "I was angry."

"I'm sorry," he whispered, "I wish I was there for you."

"You were."

Silence fell in the room and Rachel turned off the bedside lamp, enveloping them in darkness.

Much later that evening, she was still wide awake, sleep evaded her. She quietly got out of bed, put on the coat Mary had given her and snuck out of the room.

A few automobiles were scattered in the dim-lit deserted parking lot. With a few coins in her pocket she walked over to the vending machine. Yet another perk of modern technology she had come to enjoy. She fed the coins into the machine, selected her choice of a cola, but nothing happened.

Pressing the button again, she waited.

"*Ach*," she muttered as she repeatedly pushed the button.

"Here, let me," a stranger said next to her.

Startled, she jumped and stood back, fear spreading through her like wild fire.

The man banged the side of the vending machine and her cola rolled out into the feeding tray.

"These things can be quite temperamental," he murmured as he leaned against the machine.

"*Denki*," she swallowed and bent down to retrieve her cola.

His dark eyes roamed over her like a hungry beast. "A pretty girl like you shouldn't be wandering around alone in the dead of night."

"I-I'm not alone," she whispered nervously.

"No?" he glanced around, "There aint nobody else here." He switched the matchstick he was chewing from one side of his mouth to the other while flicking the lighter with his other hand. "You're not from around here are ya?"

She shook her head and sidestepped him, but he blocked her way. "Please sir," she said, "My friend is waiting for me."

"Is she now?"

"He," she corrected him. "He is waiting for me, and if I am not back soon, he will come and look for me," she lied.

"Fancy that, your man sends you out on your own, doesn't look like he's taking very good care of you."

A cold shiver ran down her spine and fear wrapped itself around her heart. With as much confidence as she could conjure up, she raised her chin and said, "I need to go."

"Why in such a hurry, we just met," he murmured and stepped closer.

*Gott, please help me...* she prayed as she stared up at the man towering above her.

"I suggest you leave the girl alone."

Relief washed over Rachel at the sound of Michael's voice. Compared to the man standing in front of her, Michael was much bigger, and she instantly felt safe.

The man raised his hands in surrender and stepped aside, "Not looking for any trouble, I was just meeting the lady's acquaintance."

Michael held out his hand, "Come on Rachel."

She scurried past the man and hurried over to Michael instantly feeling safe.

"You shouldn't run off like that," he said gripping her hand firmly as they made their way back to the room. "The city is no place for a woman, especially not a naïve girl."

She tugged her hand free and barrelled past him to their room, her face red with embarrassment and anger. And the moment they were inside, she spun around and glared at him.

"I am not naïve!" she shouted.

"Of course you are, you are inexperienced in the ways of the world, and the fact that you thought you could come to the city and start a life you have no clue about says it all," Michael blurted. "Do you know what happens to girls on the street?"

Rachel could hardly contain her anger, and with her fists balled by her sides she bit back the tears that threatened to spill. "I wasn't born yesterday!"

"No, but you were born in a small Amish village Rachel, and you don't know what's out here, whatever you think this is, it's not a game. There are evil men in this world, men who wouldn't think twice to hurt a young beautiful girl like you!"

*Beautiful...* she paused. Michael thought her to be beautiful.

He continued, "If anything had to happen to you, I would be beside myself, why do you think I came to find you? Just to punish you and drag you back to a life you hate? I came to find you because I, because I... you know what, never mind. It's late. You need to decide what it is you want." He spun around and under his breath uttered, "*Deerich* girl."

"You're a *dummkopp*, I hate you!" she screamed and ran into the bathroom, slamming the door shut.

"You have to let Gott heal your heart Rachel, it's the only way you can find peace," she heard him say before he fell silent.

He was right, she realized, she was a foolish girl. The city was no place for someone like her and the sooner she came to terms with that the better, and her only hope was perhaps turning back to Gott.

## Chapter 6

*Home*, Rachel thought as she entered the house where she grew up in, but it was nothing but four walls containing memories of a life she once cherished. Facing the Bishop and the other elders after her untimely departure right after her mother's funeral was the least of her worries. Something had happened between her and Michael that remained unresolved and if anything she wished she could take back the words she had uttered in a moment of anger.

For hours, she sat in her mamm's room, the bible lying on the small table next to the bed, exactly as her mamm had left it, contemplating her situation and searching her heart. With trembling fingers she reached for it and sighed, "Herr Gott, I miss her, so much," she prayed, "My heart is broken and I have nowhere else to turn."

She glanced down at the bible in her lap and the scripture caught her eyes.

*Psalm 34 v 18 –The Lord is near to those who are discouraged; he saves those who have lost all hope.*

Tears filled her eyes, and she wiped them away with the back of her hand. The pain and loss she had suffered had blinded her to the comfort only Gott could provide and for the first time in weeks, she realized how stubborn and ungrateful she was.

The next morning, she woke up, still curled up in her mamm's bed with the bible next to her. But the day was new and rays of sunlight spilled into the room. She had to make things right, apologize to Michael and let him know she didn't hate him.

With her mind made up she got dressed in her traditional clothes, her lilac dress, apron and *kapp*, with her hair tied up. The clothes Mary had given her lay discarded in a bag in the corner of the room, which she planned on posting back to her friend.

As she glanced at herself in the mirror, she realized just how silly she had been. This was the Rachel she knew, the girl who helped wherever she was needed. The woman her mother wanted her to be. The woman, she wanted to be.

With her head held high and her heart beating a thousand beats a second, she made her way down to the Bishop's house. This was no easy task. Chances were that he would reprimand her, or even chase her away from his house, but it was a chance she was willing to take. She took the first step up to their door, then the next, her feet feeling like lead, held her breath and knocked.

"Rachel," Bishop Fischer said as he opened the door. "I see you found your way back?"

"*Guten mariye* Bishop."

"Done *rutsching* around?" he muttered.

"I-I wanted to come by and apologize for my behaviour," she started and cleared her throat, "It was wrong and I didn't want to cause you any *druwwel*."

"*Druwwel* is the least of it; you put my wife through a lot when Michael ran after you like a love sick puppy."

Nervously, she rubbed her hands together. Bishop Fischer wasn't making this any easier, but he was right. She had caused them too much trouble and expecting them to just sweep it under the rug was unfair.

"I know. I was a *dummkopp* for running off like that."

He snickered, "You are right about that. Young women do not *shick* like loose cannons, *rutsching* around in a city they have no business with."

"*Daett*?"

It was Michael who came up behind her and she spun around.

"*Vas is letz*?" he addressed his *daett*. "Hallo Rachel."

"Hallo Michael."

"*Vie gehts*?"

"I'm good *jah*, I wanted to just come and apologize for my foolishness."

"And it's rightly so," the Bishop muttered.

"*Daett*, please, Rachel has been through enough," he countered.

The bishop's deadpanned expression unsettled her, and she turned to leave, but Michael stopped her.

"Are you not the one to preach about the Prodigal son returning? Who are we to judge Rachel?"

Rachel inhaled sharply, "Michael it's fine," she whispered.

"Nein, it is not fine, everyone deserves forgiveness."

Michael's challenged his *daett* and the Bishop's eyes narrowed before he folded his hands in front of him and his expression softened.

"Das is true my son," the Bishop said and stepped aside, "Please Rachel, come in and have some tea."

She looked at Michael who nodded, and then at the Bishop. "I would love to but I have a few things I need to do."

The Bishop smiled, "I'm sure you do, Michael why don't you go and help her?"

"No need," she protested.

"I insist," Michael grinned.

With Michael's help, Rachel had sent the parcel off to Mary, containing all the Englisch clothes, and he took her to visit her mother's grave. And as the sun was setting over the hill, they took a slow walk back to her house.

"Rachel," Michael said as they reached her house.

She held her breath, "Jah?"

"I know you see me as a friend, but I was wondering if I could pick you up for Church on Sunday?"

Her heart gave a slight flutter, "If your *daett* doesn't mind?"

Michael laughed, "He doesn't mind."

A shy smile tugged at the corners of her mouth and she nodded, "Jah, I would like that."

"Gut, I'll see you on Sunday."

"The lord is close to the broken hearted, and saves those who are crushed in spirit," she recited as she closed the door behind her. Her Gott had brought her back home, and her broken heart could finally heal.

# SAME AMISH GIRL

22

KYLIE PRICE

Ivy set the steaming pot of potatoes on the table and dropped the over mitts, waving her hands to protest the heat.

"I tried to warn you," Martha teased. "You never fail to burn your hands with the potatoes."

Ivy chuckled and shrugged.

"I suppose I am a slow learner," she agreed, smiling at her sister. "No harm done. All my fingers are accounted for."

She waved them teasingly to prove her point but her cheerfulness was quickly quashed by her mother's sharp tone.

"You are also a slow decision maker," their mother chimed in sharply as she shoved her way between her daughters to place the bread on the surface.

Both girls tensed slightly.

Liza Wittmer was not renowned for her kindness nor tact.

Under normal circumstances, the sisters would know to simply keep their distance from their surly mother but at dinnertime, it was impossible to avoid whatever tongue lashing that might be in store.

"Is something bothering you, *Mammi*?" Ivy asked, regretting the question as soon as it left her lips. She was certain that Liza's list of grievances was long and petty.

"As if you don't know," Liza snapped, spinning to glare at her oldest child. "Autumn is upon us again and once more you have neither announced your intention to be baptized nor your choice in marriage. This is becoming tiresome, Ivy."

"*Mammi,* she is in no rush," Martha said defensively. "She will do it when she is ready."

"I was not speaking to you, Martha although I have noticed you are following in your sister's footsteps quite adeptly."

Martha glowered but she did not respond.

"The time for *Rumspringa* has passed, Ivy. You have allowed yourself to fall into the trap that all beautiful girls do, wasting your youth on trivialities. I insist that you settle on someone. You cannot allow half of the district to court you. It is not proper."

Ivy rolled her eyes so only her sister could see.

"Yes, *Mammi*," she sighed, tired of the conversation already.

"What would you have her do? Simply marry for the sake of marrying?" Martha insisted and Ivy adored her for it.

Despite being two years younger, Martha had always assumed the role of the older sister somehow, jumping to Ivy's defence when Liza grew irritable.

Which was often.

Liza never let her daughters forget that she had been miserable in her choices from the day she was born.

"I would have her settle down, yes. Not everyone gets the luxury of marrying for love," Liza snapped and the girls gaped at her.

"*Mammi*!" Ivy cried. "What a thing to say! You loved *Daed*!"

But as she said it, she wasn't sure she spoke the truth.

Liza didn't respond, storming into the kitchen.

"Make sure you don't get married until you are certain you won't loathe you husband as much as *Mammi* did *Daed*," Martha whispered.

The words filled Ivy with sadness but she secretly wondered if that wasn't precisely why she hadn't agreed to marry anyone.

There was nothing wrong with the three men vying for her attention, each of them dear in their own way.

Ezekiel was hardworking and steady, Mark, witty and John had been her companion since childhood.

Each man made her happy but none of them made her heart flutter the way she had envisioned.

*Perhaps that sort of love doesn't exist outside of story books,* she often thought. After all, it had been two years of the almost tedious courtships and on some level, Ivy could understand her mother's frustration.

"Don't let *Mammi* upset you," Martha said quietly, sensing her sister's disquiet. "She only needs something about which to complain. You will marry when you are ready."

"I know," Ivy murmured but she lacked conviction in herself.

"You seem distracted today," John commented as Ivy swirled her straw around in her milkshake.

She looked up quickly and smiled faintly.

"Do I?" she asked. "I suppose I was just thinking about the farm. We had a terrible year with the drought."

John nodded.

"I know," he replied, reaching for her hand comfortingly. "But it will get better. We always get through it."

Ivy parted her lips to respond but before she could say anything, her eyes were drawn to a shiny, silver sports car pulling into the diner's lot.

Her eyes widened as am attractive man in his late twenties jumped from the driver's seat and ambled toward the entrance.

Inexplicably, Ivy felt a shiver run through her as heat flushed her fair cheeks.

"What are you looking at?" John asked, turning his head to match her gaze.

Humiliated, Ivy lowered her eyes.

"*Nichts*," she mumbled, hoping that John would not see the handsome man but it was far too late for that.

"He must be lost," John chuckled. "*Mein Gotte*, that car is bright!"

Ivy wished he had not caught her staring.

"We should go," Ivy told him, rising from her chair, gathering her long skirt with a hand so it did not snag on the table.

"Already?" he asked in surprise. "It is early yet."

"*Ja*," Ivy agreed. "But I promised Martha I would make supper tonight. She has been at market today."

"Where is Liza?"

"She has a meeting with some of the women to discuss church business," Ivy fibbed. She didn't know why she suddenly felt the urge to flee the diner but the presence of the stranger seemed to affect her mood greatly.

"Okay," John said, reluctantly rising. "I feel like I see less and less of you these days."

Ivy swallowed her guilt and smiled at him.

"I will make more time for you," she promised.

"I don't see how," John sighed. "You are so busy with your other suitors."

Ivy bristled at the mention and her green eyes narrowed slightly.

"I don't see how anything has changed in the last two years," Ivy said tersely. "But if you have an issue with Ezekiel and Mark now, I suggest you speak up."

"I have an issue with your refusing to marry me!" John retorted and Ivy's mouth parted in shock at the loudness of his tone. "Some days I feel as if I am a dog following you, hoping for a scratch behind the ears."

"Watch your voice!" she chastised him, looking around in embarrassment.

To add to her mortification, the Englischer with the fancy car was watching them intently.

"I have never refused to marry you," Ivy hissed, grabbing his arm and shooing him toward the exit. "But with the way you are speaking to me now, maybe I should have."

He wrenched his arm away from her and glared daggers in her direction.

"I have waited long enough for you, Ivy," he snapped. "It is time for me to move on!"

She gaped at him as he stormed from the diner, her heart quivering.

*He is angry with me for taking so long! I don't blame him but how can he be so harsh with his words? He has never talked to me in such a way before!*

"Are you all right, miss?"

The dashing Englischer was at her side and Ivy looked up at him almost blankly.

"What? Oh, yes."

She straightened her spine and cleared her throat, suddenly nervous at his nearness.

He seemed to have an almost hypnotic affect on her as he peered at her with intense dark eyes.

"Are you sure? You seem shaken."

"I am fine," she told him in a brusque tone.

*What business is it of yours?* She wanted to ask but she was secretly comforted by his nearness.

"Why don't you sit down with me?" he offered, gesturing to a booth behind him. "I'll buy you a cup of coffee."

She eyed him uncertainly, wanting to say yes instinctively but as she nodded, she heard herself refuse.

"No, *Danke,*" she said quickly, turning to leave.

"Another time then?" he called after her but Ivy didn't acknowledge him as she hurried out of the diner.

On the street, Ivy ducked around a corner and stopped, her pulse racing.

She paused to catch her breath but she couldn't seem to get the image of the blonde haired stranger from her mind.

*Don't be dumkupp! You have more than enough on your plate right now without bringing an Englischer into it,* she chided herself furiously.

But she could not stop thinking about the man.

It was Ivy's day to work at the market as Martha tended the fields but she was not in the mood to deal with the public.

Her encounter with John lingered in her mind and Ivy was hoping for some peace.

"You must go," Martha insisted. "I cannot bear to listen to Jonah Lapp talk about his cousin from New York for one more minute."

"What's this?" Ivy asked, only half-curious. Her mind was occupied with matters more important than the immature and chatty Jonah Lapp.

"Jonah's cousin is in Elkhart for a visit and he has not stopped talking about him since before he arrived. Hasn't he talked your ear off about him yet?"

Ivy shook her blonde braid.

"I merely stick my face in my book when I see him near," she replied, chuckling dryly. "I always fear eye contact will instigate a conversation I cannot escape."

"I must remember to bring a book with me," Martha sighed. "Can we not move booths?"

"Do you wish to ask *Mammi* about that?" Ivy joked and Martha groaned.

"I do not know which is worse; listening to Johan Lapp or *Mammi*."

They exchanged a look.

"Mammi," they agreed in unison and giggled.

Ivy rose from her spot at the kitchen table and reached for her cloak in the hall.

"I will go today," she relented. "And I will listen to Jonah speak about his cousin."

*It will be a good distraction from my own troubles,* she thought optimistically.

Jonah did not give her a moment to breathe when she arrived and she heard him prattling off about his visiting relative as she set up her wares in the market booth.

"He is so much fun," Jonah boasted. "And already successful for someone so young! He has more money than *Gotte* himself! "

"We don't care about such material things, Jonah. We are bound the *Ordnung*," Ivy reminded him gently.

"I know," he replied sullenly. "But it is interesting to see how people swoon in his presence."

Ivy could not imagine such nonsense nor did she care.

*He is exaggerating,* she thought but she didn't stop Jonah from singing praise about Jordan and she could not help but smile.

Jonah was raised as an only child and Ivy could tell how he adored his cousin.

*It does not do me any harm to listen,* she reasoned.

"Oh!" Jonah said suddenly, his face brightening more if possible. "There he is now!"

Ivy turned to look where her stand mate was pointing and her heart leapt into her throat.

It was the stranger she had met in the diner the previous afternoon.

*Well, I did not meet him exactly,* she thought, darting her eyes downward as he approached but not before she noticed his coffee colored eyes widen with recognition.

"Jordan!" Jonah called happily. "You came!"

"Hey, Jo," the blonde Englischer said pleasantly. "I warned you I was coming."

"I am so glad you're here!" Jonah gushed but Jordan's gaze was fixated on Ivy.

"Who is your friend?"

"Oh! Ivy Wittmer, this is my cousin, Jordan Lapp. Jordan, this is my friend and neighbor, Ivy."

"Very nice to meet you, Ivy."

He tried to hold her gaze as he extended a hand but Ivy ignored both.

"I must get back to work," she told Jonah quickly, turning away to hide herself inside the booth but even as she did, she knew how foolish it was; there was nowhere to hide.

She picked up her book and pretended to read but her ears were carefully trained on the conversation between the cousins next door.

It had never occurred to her that Jonah's cousin was Englisch.

*Of course you never asked either,* she told herself. Suddenly she wished she had listened more carefully to Jonah when he spoke.

"*Guder mariye, liebchen!*"

Ivy gasped as Mark poked his dark head over the counter.

"Mark! You startled me!" she laughed nervously. "What are you doing here?"

"I was on my way to see Deacon Peachery and I thought I would see if you were here today. *Mammi* asked if we can reschedule supper tonight," Mark told her apologetically. "Beth is feeling unwell and she is worried about getting everyone sick. She says she will make it up to you with a pig roast on Saturday if my sister is better."

Ivy's eyes darted up and she could feel Jordan staring at her.

"I'm sorry Beth is sick," she whispered but she was feeling immensely relieved.

After what had happened with John, she worried that it was only a matter of time before Mark and Ezekiel said the same to her.

*And then I will be all alone without any suitors because I can't make up my mind.*

Mark's brow furrowed slightly and he gazed behind him nervously before leaning further over the counter, his straw hat falling forward as he pressed his wiry chest to the wood.

"Why are you whispering?" he asked and Ivy forced a nervous smile.

"I'm not," she replied in a normal tone. "There must have been a frog in my throat."

His face registered understanding.

"All right," he said, jumping back to his feet. "Perhaps we can go for a walk after supper then?"

"I will call on you if I can," she told him quickly, her face flushing crimson. "I won't come in the house."

Jordan's eyes seemed to be burning a hole into her.

"Sounds *guder, liebling.* See you later," Mark told her and Ivy nodded, watching as he wandered away.

"It sounds as if you are free for supper tonight," Jordan said, approaching the booth. Jonah was busy with customers.

"You should not be listening to other people's conversations," she said sternly. "It's rude."

"Your boyfriend shouldn't be so loud then," Jordan laughed. He continued to stare at her.

"Why are you looking at me like that?" Ivy demanded, trying to hide her face but it was an exercise in futility.

"I am waiting for an answer to my question," he replied. "Will you have supper with me tonight?"

Ivy studied his face, wondering what it was specifically about him which she found so magnetic.

It was more than his simple good looks.

His blonde hair was thick but kept short in an attractive crew cut and his brown eyes sparkled against his olive complexion.

*He is a man who enjoys being in the sun,* she thought, trying not to openly examine the rest of his broad frame.

Many men were attractive, possibly even more so than Jordan but no other man caused her heart to pound the way he seemed to so effortlessly.

"A quick meal," Ivy relented.

*Mammi already believes that I am going to Mark's for supper tonight. I will not have to explain myself to anyone when this goes awry,* she thought.

Again, her pulse seemed to race as Jordan's face exploded into a genuine smile of happiness.

"Where can I pick you up?" he asked and Ivy shook her head.

"I will meet you," she told him and Jordan's ebon eyes glinted with understanding.

"Of course," he agreed. "Le Chat Noir on East Bristol? Six o'clock?"

Ivy swallowed, not trusting her voice as she nodded in agreement.

"Perfect!" he exclaimed. "I can't wait!"

Jordan winked happily at her before turning back to his cousin.

*Oh no,* Ivy thought, gnawing on her lip. *Why did I agree to that?*

But no matter how hard she tried, she couldn't help but be excited for the impending date.

As she was closing the stall that evening, Ivy had yet another unexpected visitor.

"John!" she gasped. "What are you doing here?"

Her head was becoming dizzy from all of the men flittering through the marketplace that day.

He approached her sheepishly, hanging his head in shame.

"I acted like a fool yesterday, Ivy," he told her quietly. "I am here to apologize."

She eyed him warily.

"You only said how you felt," she replied evenly. "I just wish you hadn't said it so loudly."

He nodded in agreement.

"I am just desperate to start my life with you, Ivy. Everyone knows you are the most desired woman in the district and I constantly live in fear that I will lose you to someone else."

Ivy smiled patiently at him.

"I know you are growing impatient," she replied. "And I'm sorry I am the cause of that but I do not wish to commit to marriage until I am certain."

"I know!" John grumbled. "I just wish you were certain already!"

Ivy laughed and kissed him quickly on the cheek.

"I must go now but we will talk later, *ja?*"

He nodded but Ivy could see that he was reluctant to let her go.

*For the first time,* she thought nervously as she hurried to meet Jordan. *He might have something to genuinely worry about.*

A small part of her had hoped that the dinner would be disastrous and that Jordan would prove to be less stimulating than he appeared.

Yet as the evening progressed, Ivy felt herself enthralled by everything the man did.

She learned he was a surgeon at a private hospital in New York, specializing in work with children and the knowledge only made Ivy more attracted to him.

*This is impossible,* Ivy told herself as she studied the curve of his cheekbones. *We have no future together and you have enough suitors. Bid him goodnight and forget about whatever is going on in your stomach.*

It proved to be easier thought than done and when Jordan escorted her back to her wagon after their meal of lobster and crème brule, neither which Ivy had ever tasted before.

She felt much like a princess when he walked with her.

"Ivy..."

"*Danke* for a lovely supper," she interjected quickly as if sensing he was going to say something she was not prepared to hear. "I hope you enjoy the rest of your stay here in Elkhart – "

"Ivy, why are you denying the electricity between us?" he interrupted, determined to say what he wanted to say.

A hot blush rose up her chest and she lowered her eyes.

"*Danke,*" she mumbled again, unsure of what else to say.

She turned toward her cart.

"Please have dinner with me again tomorrow," he pleaded, grabbing for her arm as she turned.

Ivy gazed back at him, fighting the urge to kiss him.

*This is so strange,* she thought, shaking her head in disbelief. *I have never felt like this with anyone before.*

"Yes," she finally managed to say. "I will have supper with you."

He exhaled as if he had been holding his breath dependant on her answer.

"Can I pick you up?" he asked and Ivy thought of what her mother would say if she brought an Englischer home.

"No," she replied quickly. "I will meet you at the market."

He looked disappointed but he nodded.

"I look forward to it," he told her and Ivy could read the earnestness in his eyes.

She jumped onto the bench of her cart and rode away before she could succumb to the desire in her heart.

*You have been looking for a man who instills this reaction in you,* she reminded herself as she made her way back home. *Why did it have to be an Englischer?*

She was a mass of confused emotions as she steered the cart up the long drive toward the farmhouse but as she approached, she saw Martha standing on the porch with her mother and Ezekiel.

*What is he doing here?* She wondered, her mind racing. *Was I to meet him tonight?*

She didn't think so but she couldn't reconcile why he would be at the house unannounced.

"Where have you been?" Liza yelled as he disembarked.

"I was at dinner," Ivy answered truthfully but Liza's scowl only deepened.

"Not with Mark," she snarled and Ivy wondered how she could know already.

"Ezekiel, what are you doing here?" she asked and his brow furled into a frown so tight, she almost couldn't see his eyes.

"Mark was found in a ditch this afternoon. A hit and run."

The hospital would tell her nothing as she was not family but from what Mark's mother, Rachel explained, he was in critical condition.

"How did this happen?" Ivy moaned, her heart filled with pain.

*We were going to go for a walk tonight,* she thought. *Weren't we?*

More guilt consumed her as she thought of how she was off enjoying dinner with Jordan while her suitor lay alone.

"There is nothing you can do here tonight," Rachel told her. "Go home and I will send word if there is any change."

Ivy did not want to leave but she could see that Rachel did not wish for her to be there any longer.

Devastated, she returned to the district and into Ezekiel's arms.

"This is terrible," she whispered and he comforted her the best way he knew how, allowing her to rest her head on his shoulder as they sat in the yard, staring up at the stunningly clear night.

But it felt strange, touching Ezekiel and Ivy pulled herself away.

"I should retire," she sighed after a long period of silence. "I am to tend the farm tomorrow."

Ezekiel nodded and rose, dusting his pants off.

"I will let you know if I hear anything about Mark," he told her gently and she nodded gratefully.

She went inside and laboriously climbed the stairs to the second floor, her heart heavy.

*What a terrible accident,* she thought, swallowing her tears. *I hope they find whoever is responsible.*

Ivy was understandably distracted the following day and she barely noticed when a shiny silver car appeared in front of the house until Liza came searching for her, green eyes blazing with anger.

"There is a man here looking for you," she spat. "An Englischer."

Ivy looked up from the crops in shock, her head jerking to look toward the house.

Jordan stood, his hand acting as a visor as he stared at her.

Even from the distance between them, Ivy could make out the smile on his face.

*Oh no,* she thought worriedly, hurrying to greet him but she could feel her mother's eyes boring into her back.

She knew she would hear about it later from her mother but Ivy was secretly pleased to see Jordan.

"What are you doing here?" she gasped at him. "You should not have come. My midder..."

"I had to see you," Jordan interrupted. "I heard about your friend Mark and I wanted to see how you were doing."

Ivy blinked.

"Oh."

She studied his face, aware that Liza was quickly approaching.

"You should go," she told him urgently, not wanting her mother to have the opportunity to question him before she time to properly prepare him.

"Are you sure?" he asked as Ivy ushered him toward his car. "Are we still meeting tonight?"

She nodded quickly.

"Yes," she replied. "But please, go now."

He gazed back at her reluctantly but nodded and slipped into his car as Liza arrived.

Ivy turned away.

"Who was that?" she demanded.

"No one," Ivy replied, rushing off before her mother could ask anything further.

But as she returned to her work in the field, Ivy could not stop the questions from filling her mind.

*How had Jordan heard about Mark?*

John met her on the road to the market that evening when she went to meet Jordan for supper.

"Have you heard anything about Mark?" he asked and Ivy stared at him for a long moment.

"No," she replied slowly. "He is still unconscious."

"This happens far too often," John muttered. "The town should do something about the speeds which people drive in these parts. Are you heading into Elkhart now?"

"Yes," Ivy replied.

"May I take a ride? I must pick up some supplies for my father. It will be easier if I go now."

Ivy gulped but she could think of no reason to refuse his request.

"All right," she sighed, hoping that he would not cross paths with Jordan.

*Oh, this is all becoming too secretive. I do not like this at all.*

But Ivy could see no easy way out of her predicament.

*I suppose I could simply tell the truth,* she thought wryly. But she wasn't sure she was ready to do that.

*After one dinner, how can you know anything?* She thought, shaking her head as they made their way toward town.

Still, she could not deny the emotions which Jordan invoked in her.

She arrived at the market and John jumped from the bench.

"Should we meet for supper?" he asked and Ivy shook her head, seeing Jordan's silver car pulling into the market lot.

"I have plans," she murmured as Jordan and Jonah jumped from the sport's car.

John turned to look, his eyes narrowing.

"With Jonah Lapp?" he asked, confused but Ivy shook her head as Jordan joined them.

"Hello," Jordan said pleasantly. "I'm Jordan Lapp."

To Ivy's shock, he slipped his arm possessively around her waist.

John's mouth parted but no sound escaped.

"Come on, Ivy," Jordan continued. "I have reservations at El Mariachi. I hope you like Mexican food."

Before she could say anything, she was swept around and led to his car as Jonah waved, disappearing into the market.

Ivy peeked at John through the windshield as Jordan climbed into the driver's seat and saw his look of disbelief but Ivy was still tingling from Jordan's touch.

It was another incredible dinner and Ivy couldn't remember precisely what they spoke of but she found herself lost in Jordan's eyes.

She temporarily forgot about Mark and her mother and everything else which had been troubling her.

*This is real,* she thought, her heart full of adoration for the Englischer. *I cannot fight it. He has a hold on me which I have never known.*

When they parted, Jordan kissed her sweetly on the cheek.

"I have decided to extend my stay," he told her.

A flutter of joy seized her but it was mixed with uncertainty.

"For how long?" she asked and he smiled.

"For as long as it takes to convince you that we are meant to be together," he replied quietly.

The words sent pleasure through Ivy and she was almost floating as she made her way into the farmhouse that night.

Liza was livid, pacing the front hall when Ivy entered.

"You were with that Englischer, weren't you?" she screamed, her face red with ire.

"*Mammi,* I am tired," she said, trying to brush past her mother but Liza reached out to grab her arm furiously.

"You are not going anywhere!" she raged.

Ivy yanked her arm away, her good mood vanishing.

"Why can't you be happy for me?" she cried. "Would you rather I chose a loveless union like you had with *Daed*?"

Liza's complexion waned.

"I would rather you worried about what is happening under your own nose. You don't see what this man is doing? You are being manipulated and you are too *dumkupp* to see it!"

Ivy stared at her.

"What are you talking about, *Mamm*?" she snapped. "You don't even know him!"

"I know that since he has come around, bad things have occurred. Do you think that is a coincidence?"

"*Mammi,* Mark was in an accident! It is terrible but it happens frequently," she snapped exasperated as Martha hurried down the stairs, hearing the commotion.

Liza's mouth curled into a cruel smile.

"And what of John?" she snarled. "Was he an accident too?"

Ivy glanced at Martha uncomprehendingly.

"John?" she echoed. "I only saw him a few hours ago. Nothing has happened to John."

Martha shook her head, lowering her eyes.

"John is very sick, Ivy," she murmured. "He was admitted to the hospital not long ago."

"That's impossible," Ivy decried. "I only just saw him and he was perfectly well."

Martha sighed as Liza snorted in disgust.

"No," Martha replied. "The doctor says he was poisoned."

Ivy could not make sense of what was happening but something was clear; her suitors were being targeted.

Jordan's words, ones that had once filled her with such elation suddenly had a terrifying undertone.

*"I have decided to extend my stay...for as long as it takes to convince you that we are meant to be together."*

Ivy could not believe that she had been so deluded by Jordan's charms that she had not seen the evil in him.

But try as she might, she couldn't believe that the man she had grown to know over the past days had such malice in his bones.

*You had no business getting involved with such a man,* she told herself angrily. *You could not have been happy with what you had and you endangered people because of it. You do not know the first thing about Jordan Lapp.*

All Ivy knew was that she had to keep her distance before something happened to Ezekiel too.

Ivy stayed close to the farm for the next few days, carefully avoiding Jordan who came calling.

For the first time, Ivy was grateful for her mother's harsh ways. She kept the man at bay, despite his repeated attempts to contact her.

Martha took her to visit John and Mark in the hospital, carefully hiding her in the wagon under a blanket just in case Jordan was watching for her.

"Hopefully he will return to New York soon," Martha told her one evening as they arrived at Elkhart General Hospital. "He cannot stay here forever."

Ivy did not respond. She didn't want to tell her sister that she had her doubts about Jordan's guilt in the incidents, no matter how suspicious it seemed.

She felt that Martha would not understand.

*If I were Martha and Mammi, I would not understand either but what if it is all a terrible coincidence?*

It was a risk she could not afford to take, she knew that logically but her heart would not let go of the idea that she was meant to be with Jordan.

*You must forget about him,* she told herself firmly, climbing the stairs to the intensive care unit.

John had been asleep when she had tried visiting there first and Martha had slipped away to the cafeteria to get a cup of coffee.

"I will let you speak with Rachel alone," Martha told her. "I will meet you in the front when you have finished."

Gratefully, Ivy had agreed.

She felt as if Martha was a witness to the shame she had brought to the district, despite the fact that her sister had been nothing but supportive.

As Ivy approached the landing, she gasped in shock.

Jordan was standing in the stairwell on his cell phone.

As if he sensed her there, he spun to stare at her.

"I will call you back. Email me that list of specialists," he told the caller, disconnecting his call.

"Why are you here?" Ivy breathed, a wave of dizziness overcoming her.

"Why have you been avoiding me?" he replied, his face a mask of confusion. "Are you angry with me?"

*How can he act so innocently? He knows what he has done.*

"I cannot speak with you right now," Ivy mumbled, brushing past him to reach for the door.

"Ivy, please talk to me! Why did you suddenly cut me off? I thought we had a special connection!"

"So did I!" she cried before she could stop herself. "Why did you hurt John and Mark? Are you going after Ezekiel next?"

He gaped at her, his brown eyes filled with consternation and then flooded with understanding.

"You – you think I had something to do with what happened?" he gasped. "I would never!"

The expression of hurt and anger on his face was convincing but Ivy knew she could not simply accept his claim.

"Why are you here if you have nothing to do with it?" she demanded, crossing her arms over her chest. "You have no right to be here!"

Jordan's mouth parted.

"I am here with my cousin," he replied gruffly. "I am a surgeon in New York and I was speaking with some of colleagues about Mark's situation."

Ivy's eyes narrowed.

*Why was Jonah here? He and Mark have never been friends.*

Before she could poise the question, the door flew inward, almost knocking them both over.

"Jordan," Jonah gasped. "We must go."

His face went waxen as he saw Ivy.

Jordan shook his head.

"Not yet," he told his cousin firmly. "Ivy and I are having a conversation."

"No!" Jonah choked. "We must go immediately! Mark is awake!"

Ivy's eyes grew wide as she and Jordan stared at him.

"That's wonderful!" she gasped, rushing past Jonah.

Rachel stood talking animatedly with a doctor, relief coloring her face but as she neared, Mark's mother's face turned stony as the physician continued to speak.

Slowly, the woman turned her head, her face pinched into a look of sheer fury and Ivy felt her blood run cold.

"You!" she spat and Ivy froze in her tracks. "How could you? He was your friend!"

Ivy stared at her uncomprehendingly but before she could respond, two security officers appeared in the hallway.

"Right there!" the doctor called. "The Amish one."

Ivy was stone still as the guards rushed toward her.

They passed her in a whoosh of air and Ivy whirled to see where they had gone.

"No!" Jonah screamed. "Don't touch me! I didn't do anything!"

"That is not what the patient is saying," Dr. Andrews intoned. "Mark is awake and he remembers it was you who hit him."

Jordan stared at his cousin in shock.

"Jonah?" he breathed. "Did you hit him and leave the scene?"

"No!" Jonah yelled but Ivy could see the guilt on his face.

"Why?" Ivy demanded. "Why would you do such a terrible thing?"

"Because you are too silly to see my cousin is the one you should be with!" Jonah roared. "He is better than Mark or John or Ezekiel. He is better than any of the men in this town!"

"Oh Jonah," Jordan moaned. "What did you do?"

"I was only helping you get what you want, Jordan. You love Ivy. I can tell. If everyone else was out of the way..."

"Take him to the office to wait for the police," Dr. Andrews called and the guards hauled him away but Jonah was not finished talking.

"You could say thank you!" he yelled at his cousin. "I did you a favor!"

Jordan hung his head in shame as Ivy rushed to his side.

"I had no idea," he murmured. "How could I have known he was so unbalanced?"

"You could not have known," Ivy replied reassuringly. "It is not your fault."

"Isn't it?" Jordan asked bitterly. "I should have known better than to interfere with your ways and customs. I shouldn't have pursued you."

Ivy reached up to touch his face, shaking her blonde head vehemently.

"I am glad you pursued," she whispered. "And I am sorry I suspected you of such an awful thing."

He peered into her eyes, his dark irises clashing with her green ones.

"I don't blame you," he sighed begrudgingly. "I think if the roles were reversed, I would have had my doubts too."

They smiled at one another for a long moment.

"We should check on Mark," he told her and she nodded but as he went to move, she grabbed his arm and cupped his cheeks in her hands.

"Are you free for supper tonight?" she asked.

Jordan half-smiled.

"Where should we meet?" he asked warily but Ivy shook her head.

"I was thinking that you come to my house and meet my family," she told him.

Jordan's eyes brightened and a smile lit his face.

"I would like that," he agreed.

Ivy pulled his face toward hers and kissed him gently on the lips.

*This is everything I have ever wanted. I am not fighting it any longer...no matter what Mammi has to say.*

# UNCOMMON AMISH GROUND

44

MONICA MARKS

"Father, please don't –!"

The plea came too late and was unheeded as a bucket of cold water was released onto Emilia's head, about her bonnet and down along the front of her dress.

"Father!" she screamed, furiously. "Why on earth would you do such a thing!"

Jumping from her chair, she whirled around to face him, her brown eyes flashing with anger. To her dismay, he was beaming as if he had bestowed some act of kindness upon her.

"Emilia, it is summertime! You are cooped up within the walls of a house, knitting a sweater," he replied, reaching out to take her arm. "I do believe that the sunshine is calling your name."

"A sweater that is now ruined!" Emilia complained but allowed for Abel to lead her from the dark stone house into the yard, dripping water heavily along the way. Her two younger sisters were engaged in a game of hopscotch on the road, their long braids flailing in the wind.

"You see? Even the children know better than to stay indoors when the day is fraught with beauty. What kind of example are you setting for the young ones?"

"Father, I do not have time for trivial tasks. I needed to have that sweater finished for the marketplace. After which I have to begin making supper. Now I will be up half the night knitting!"

"Ah! One less sweater at the marketplace will not be the end of days. Also, you do not have to make supper tonight. We have been invited to the home of our neighbor." Emilia turned and looked at him suspiciously at the sudden announcement.

"Which neighbor?" she demanded. Again, Abel smiled, undaunted by his eldest daughter's scrutiny.

"The new members of our community. They reside only a few houses down the road."

"Father, you don't mean that sour faced man with the sullen little girl, do you? I did not like the looks of those two at church. They seem to not like being here. We don't know anything about them."

"My dear, you do not like the look of anyone. That is because you don't truly look at anyone. And that is why we are going this evening; to learn about them and make them feel welcome. "

"Oh father, that is simply not accurate. I do not engage in silliness like other women. I much prefer my own company to idle chit chat. There is no harm in that. I believe it shows that I have a strong head on my shoulders."

"Indeed, it does, my daughter. Once in a while, however, you can relax and enjoy the sunshine." Emilia did not reply. This was an old argument. Since the passing of her mother six years earlier, Abel Troyer had done his best to keep his three daughters in high spirits. The two youngest had eventually moved on from the unexpected death but Emilia had clung to the memory of her mother like a spider web shawl, refusing to let light into her life. Abel desperately missed the infectious sound of Emilia's laughter, a tone which used to ring through the hills of their community like a tinkling bell.

"Regardless, father, I see no reason why we should join Mr. Bawell and his daughter for supper," Emilia finally said. "But if you feel you must, by all means, do go without me."

"It is my wish that we attend supper at their residence and so we shall. I am still the head of this household, Emilia. I do not appreciate being contradicted." Abel was beginning to lose his good humor. He did not understand why everything had to be a fight with Emilia. When his wife had been alive, Emilia had been the model child, obedient and respectful. He knew she only wanted to be left alone to her brooding but he would not have it. She was perfectly healthy, a lovely, kind hearted woman who deserved happiness. It was his job as her father to ensure that she received it. Emilia wisely closed her mouth and turned to face her siblings as her father walked off into the back part of the yard, seeming to have no more interest in teasing his child.

"Emmy, will you play with us?" Collette called, her blonde hair almost white in the droplets of sunlight. Emilia forced herself to smile and shook her head. For a fleeting moment, she was tempted to join the children but she pushed the thought from her mind.

"Not today, Collette. I have work to do."

"You always have work to do, Emmy!" Evelyn pouted. Collette took her younger sister's hand and pulled the nine-year-old toward the veranda.

"She is busy taking care of us, Evie. We are going to mammi and dawdy's now anyway. We must get dressed."

"Wait one moment, Collette. You're going to mammi and dawdy's house? Father just said that we are going to our new neighbor's for supper. Are you certain?"

Collette paused at the door to allow Evelyn to pass.

"You and papa are going to Aaron Bawell's for supper. Evie and I are going to mammi and dawdy's." The girls disappeared into the house and Emilia was left on the porch, still dripping from her father's cold water bath. She narrowed her smoky eyes. *Why is he sending Evie and Collette to our grandparents' house? What is papa up to?* She cringed inwardly as she had her suspicions.

"Emilia, why do you insist on being so stubborn?"

"What is it, father? What have I done now?"

Abel sighed heavily and stared at his daughter as she descended the stairs from her bedroom.

"You know full well that you cannot attend this supper wearing working clothes. Please change into more appropriate attire." Emilia blinked her solemn eyes at him.

"But father, I believed this to be work." Abel scowled and pointed firmly up the staircase.

"You will do as I say immediately, Emilia. And that is quite enough of your impudence for one day." Emilia hung her head in shame, immediately reading her father's anger and slightly stung by his words. Abel was not one to raise his voice in anger.

"Yes father. I'm sorry." She hurried back up to change her clothes and wondered why she had performed such a defiant act. She knew that her father would not have allowed her to visit the Bawell house dressed in rags. It was disrespectful. Lately she had been feeling more and more feisty and if she was not already well into her late twenties, she would have thought that she was due to experience rumspringa. She had briefly experimented with cigarettes and beer when she was younger but she had since been baptized and was very happy in the community. Well, as happy as Emilia could be. There was an unsurmountable void which had filled Emilia since the death of her young mother. She was eternally grateful for the consistency and love given by Abel, however, Emilia and her mother had a bond that seemed to outlive death. Time did not heal her pain and eventually Emilia had succumbed to the fact that she was destined to be discontent for the remainder of her life. Yet lately, the sorrow had turned into some sort of boiling anger and no matter how Emilia tried, she could not seem to tame the beast which was growing within her.

Moments later, she was descending the stairs in a freshly ironed dark blue dress, a starch white bonnet covering her thick head of hair. Abel beamed happily.

"You look lovely. Much better. Shall we?" He offered his arm to his daughter and they started out the door.

"Father, why have you sent the children to mammi and dawdy's this evening?"

"Ah because this evening is for the older people, my dear daughter." Emilia swallowed a knowing grunt but said nothing. As they strolled up the walkway toward the Bawell household, the front door flew open and Emilia was facing the petulant stare of a six-year-old child. Her blue eyes looked like frosted panes of glass as she took in the sight of the two strangers on the porch.

"Good evening, Amity," Abel boomed amiably. "How are you this fine night?"

The girl did not respond and instead turned and disappeared out of view. Emilia gave her father a look but the older man did not meet her eyes. A moment later, Aaron Bawell appeared at the door.

"Please, come in," he said, extending the front door for them to enter. Abel smiled and nodding his thanks while Emilia reluctantly followed.

"May I introduce my daughter, Emilia?" Abel said, removing hat and gesturing toward Emilia.

"Yes," Aaron replied nodding and closing the door. Emilia was slightly taken aback by his disinterested response. In her grief, Emilia had not been interested in the prospect of marriage despite her father's endless prompting.

"It is not healthy for a woman to go through life without a companion, Emilia," Abel had told her countless times. "What of children?"

"I have two daughters in Evelyn and Collette," she had replied, only half jokingly. She had not the stomach to think of child bearing when her own mother had not had the chance to watch her daughters grow up. Eventually, Abel had forsaken the quest to marry off his oldest daughter. However, she had more callers than anyone else in her community and the reason for that was simple. She was the ideal wife. She was hard working, compassionate and a deep thinker. She possessed patience and everyone was a friend to her. Also, she was incredibly lovely, with long honey blonde hair and wide, innocent brown eyes, framed in long eyelashes. Whenever Emilia flashed an elusive smile, the entire world seemed to follow her lead. Even after years of rejecting suitor after suitor, they still came knocking on her door, eager to see her wed to them.

This is why Aaron Bawell's abrupt greeting was so stunning to Emilia. He was apparently unimpressed by Emilia's presence. *He does not know you,* Emilia reasoned, following the men into the sitting room. *He has only been in our district for two weeks. He has no reason to give you a second look.* Even as Emilia thought the words, she felt a strange pang of longing. She oddly wished him to look at her again. And again. *You must stop thinking this way!* She chided herself. *Your thoughts are that of a child in puppy love!* But Emilia could not stop staring at the newcomer and taking in all the details of his strong physique. His voice was deep and mellifluous and Emilia thought she could listen to him speak all day long. She felt a blush color her cheeks and she wondered what it was about Aaron which set him apart from the others who had bid for her hand in marriage. Certainly he was handsome but many men could claim the same. He donned a beard, an indication that he was married but there had been no mention of a mother for his young daughter. Emilia suddenly realized that she was very interested in learning more about the man in whose house she sat. Aaron and Abel were having a conversation of which Emilia heard none. As they finished speaking, Aaron looked about the room, somewhat confused.

"Amity!" Aaron called out. "Join us, please."

His demand was met with no response and sighing heavily after a moment, Aaron rose to his feet.

"Excuse me," he apologized before disappearing into the home. Emilia listened as his footsteps ascended up the staircase.

"Father, what on earth are we doing here?" Emilia asked, feeling distinctly uncomfortable. Abel gave her a sidelong look and smiled briefly.

"I believe you know what we are doing her, Emilia. Aaron Bawell is a successful carpenter. He is new to the community and has not been swayed by your endless rejection. He will be a perfect match for you."

"Father!" Emilia groaned. "I had hoped you had stopped with this matchmaking foolishness long ago."

"Emilia, it is not foolishness to want your children to be happy and begin a family. You are not going to be a young woman forever, child. You must consider your future."

"Father, I – "her words were cut short as Aaron returned to the sitting room, almost dragging along his daughter.

"Papa, I don't want them to be here," Amity Bawell snarled, glaring viciously at the strangers in her living room. Against the flickering kerosene lanterns, she almost looked diabolical, her small upper lip curled above her teeth, blue eyes aflame. She was otherwise a very pretty child, a spitting image of her father. She had long, straight black hair and cornflower blue eyes. Her features were softer, less defined than Aaron with his high cheekbones but she also had the extra fat of a small child.

"You will mind your manners!" Aaron snapped back, shooting an embarrassed look toward Abel.

"I do not like you!" Amity yelled, hands on her hips, addressing Emilia. Emilia was shocked by the defiance in the girl. She could not imagine either of her sisters ever speaking in such a way. *I don't believe I am overly fond of you either, little devil,* Emilia thought, narrowing her eyes at the child.

"Amity! You will stop this insolence immediately!" Aaron thundered, rising to his feet once more. "We are in the presence of guests. Your mother would be ashamed of your behavior!"

As if her father had physically struck her, Amity seemed to crumble to the floor. Her face went waxen and her eyes filled with tears. The deviousness evaporated and suddenly Emilia was staring at an ashen faced child. For a moment, she felt her heart crack. She had never seen a sorrier sight. Amity opened her mouth as if she were about to speak but no words fluttered from her small, pink lips. Then, tears streaked her chubby face and she ran, sobbing, from the room. Heavily,

Aaron reclaimed his seat beside Abel. There was an awkward silence as everyone searched for the right words to speak. Finally, Abel cleared his throat, standing.

"We will call another time, Aaron," Emilia's father said magnanimously, ushering Emilia to her feet. "Young girls can have their bad days. I understand. I have three of them."

Abel put a smile to his statement to ease the younger man's discomfort but Aaron looked devastated, his deep blue eyes troubled and full.

"Every day is a bad day." He seemed to have heard the way his words sounded and he quickly rose to his feet.

"I apologize. I thought we had been here long enough for her to accept visitors. This transition has been extremely difficult on Amity." Aaron looked imploringly at Abel for understanding, completely ignoring Emilia. Inwardly she was shaking her head. *You are far too soft on the child. You should not make excuses,* Emilia thought. *These people are not the right fit for this community. We do not rear our children to act so recklessly.*

"Of course it has! She is but a small girl. She cannot be expected to understand so much change in so little time," Abel assured him. "Give her time."

"I will speak to the Bishop about her," Aaron promised, ushering them toward the door. "Once more, please forgive this disruption. I will reschedule our meal for another time."

"Please, do not worry. Perhaps next time you will visit with us. Evelyn is only a few years older than Amity. A friend may do her a world of good." Aaron looked thoughtful at the suggestion and nodded. The men bid each other adieu and Aaron closed the door in their wake without so much as a glance at Emilia. Again, she was stunned by his rudeness. Abel took Emilia's arm and guided her down the path leading to their modest house moments down the road. When she was quite sure they were out of earshot, Emilia turned to her father.

"Lord above, I have never seen such an ill behaved child in all of my life!" she exploded. "And that man, he's rude – "

"Emilia – "Abel attempted to cut her off but she was not finished.

"He barely spoke one full word to me. I see that the apple does not fall far from the tree! Can you imagine raising a child so willful – "

"Emilia – "

"And you, you father, why on God's green earth would you ever consider him a match for me?"

"Are you quite finished with your diatribe?" Abel asked tiredly, releasing her arm as they approached their house.

"You can't say that you weren't shocked at her behavior, father," Emilia said, baffled by his calm demeanor.

"I was not," Abel replied. Emilia arched an eyebrow, her brown eyes cynical.

"How not?"

"I was not surprised because you and your sisters behaved very similarly after your mother passed also." A wave of dizziness overwhelmed Emilia as his words set in, instantly followed by deep regret.

"You mean to tell me that Amity's mother has recently passed away?" she whispered.

"Yes. Not three weeks ago. That is why Aaron has uprooted his life and started fresh here. Amity could not bear to be in their home without her mother. He is doing his best for his daughter. You could stand to be more empathetic, daughter. You know better than anyone how difficult a time this is for someone in their position."

Emilia paused on the veranda, staring after her father. Slowly, she turned to stare up into the dusky sky. Her heart was heavy with sadness but for the first time since she could remember, the woe she felt was not for herself but for the small girl missing her mother and the man who could not take her pain away.

**II**

The following morning, Emilia dressed and fed her sisters before delivering them to their school. Their morning chatter was often the highlight of Emilia's day but that dawn, she could not get the sight of Amity Bawell's anguished blue eyes out of her head as if they were etched into her skull. Oh how she understood the poor child's misery and she desperately wished that there was a way to help the girl overcome her fresh loss. Of course, she knew from personal experience that there was no such way. The Bishop would tell her that time, family and community would help expel the pain but Emilia knew that was a lie he would tell everyone. Over and above that, Emilia found her mind traveling to Aaron's Bawell. He was still such a young man to be widowed. Abel had informed her that they had been wed eight years when cancer claimed Aaron's wife, Beth. She had been sickly for a very long while before finally succumbing to her grave. Amity had watched her mother wither away before her eyes and when she finally did go to her final rest, Aaron had immediately acted, taking Amity away from the horrible memories and the house in which her mother had suffered so greatly.

"No child should ever have to see their parent in a state like that," Able had said sadly. "Especially one so young. They cannot begin to reconcile what is happening. In a way, it is a blessing that your mother was take so quickly. She was never in agony which you girls had to witness."

Emilia swallowed the lump in her throat and nodded but she wasn't sure if she agreed. *Maybe mama wasn't in agony but we were. And some of us still are.* Emilia forced herself to think about Aaron and Amity. She vowed that she would befriend the newcomers at once. It would not make their life more bearable but it would help shoulder the burden they were carrying. The Bishop had been right about one thing; community and family did assist the process somewhat.

After sending the children off and promising to pick them up that afternoon, Emilia carefully constructed a basket of wicker and filled it with several thought-filled items. There was a freshly knit blanket she had intended to sell at the market, jars of preserves and honey, a mutton pie and a bouquet of wildflowers. She gently wrapped the basket in another wool blanket and carried the package outside and down the laneway. There was a charged nervousness about her as she knocked on the door to the Bawell house. There was no sign of movement from within the walls but the curtains were drawn. Emilia knocked again but to her disappointment, there was no response. *Ah, well I imagine Amity is in school and Aaron is off at work although Lord knows they should be home in their grief. I will just leave this here. I did not pen a note. Maybe I will run home, write a note and bring it back.* Emilia set the gift down on the small porch and was on her way to retrieve a pen and paper. Suddenly, one of the straps to her bonnet came loose and just before a short wind carried it off, Emilia reached up and snatched it back, her whole body turning. Lowering herself from the balls of her feet, she realized she was facing the Bawell house again. Aaron Bawell was standing at the door, staring at her strangely. He was wearing only a white cotton undershirt and a pair of trousers, his beard unkempt and his feet were bare. Even so, he looked incredibly handsome, his black hair a disheveled mess about his finely lined face. He looked down at the basket on the porch and then back to Emilia. She offered him a timid smile.

"My family sent you some goods to help you along," she called out. Again, his steely blue eyes looked at the package. Without a word, he turned and slammed the door behind him, leaving the present on the dusty deck.

"You must not be offended, daughter. He is grieving," Abel told Emilia when she reiterated what happened.

"I know he is grieving, father but even you have to admit that it was unfathomably rude!" Abel shrugged nonchalantly and took a sip of his tea.

"You must not forsake them in their time of need, Emilia. People often are the most trying during their darkest hour of need. It is God's way of testing you to see if you are capable of maintain humility and patience. Also, Aaron has agreed to come here for supper tomorrow evening." Emilia dropped her parring knife and stared at her father in disbelief.

"Oh father, you must stop beating a dead horse! You cannot believe that a recently widowed man is someone whom is interested in marrying your spinster daughter." Abel looked up sharply at her.

"Firstly, you are not a spinster. Not for the time being, mind you...and secondly, it is not my intention to push marriage upon a devastated man. I am merely suggesting you provide comfort to a man and a child who desperately require a support system. Everything is not sordid and dark, Emilia. You must learn that every cloud had a silver lining. And when you learn that, perhaps you can pass that information along to the Bawells." Contritely, Emilia looked at her hands and then continued peeling potatoes. Secretly she was pleased that Aaron and Amity were coming. She had been unable to stop thinking about the man, despite his brusque nature. *He is a hard man to reach, perhaps due to the circumstances.*

"Yes, father," she replied. "What shall I make for supper tomorrow night?"

"Well apparently anything but mutton," Abel jested lightly.

When Aaron and Amity appeared on the veranda of the Troyer home, something seemed different. Amity was no long sulky and angry. She was very quiet and seemed almost out of touch with what was occurring in her presence. Abel introduced her to Evelyn and Collette but she was as disinterested in the girls as Aaron was in Emilia. The entire grouping was a fiasco and Emilia wanted to escape. As the men and children sipped on lemonade on the porch, Emilia put the finishing touches on supper before calling everyone inside. The men seated at both ends of the table, grace was said and Emilia began to serve generous portions of fried beef cutlets, roasted potatoes and corn. Collette passed bread around the table.

"This is excellent, Emilia. You are a wonderful cook," Abel declared, taking a bite of his meal. She smiled at his transparency and he winked subtly in her direction.

"Thank you, father," she replied. She looked expectantly at Aaron but he continued to eat his food, unspeaking. Emilia felt her heart sink. She was expecting too much from this man. She did not know why she felt so drawn to him, why it was so important that he like her but she could not think of anything she wanted more than for him to look at her and say one kind word. Emilia sighed and put her fork onto her plate, her appetite suddenly depleted. She waited for the others to finish their meal before rising to clear away the dishes. Collette and Evelyn rose to help. When the three siblings were in the kitchen, Collette rolled her dark eyes heavenward.

"What a bore!" she exclaimed.

"Shhh!" Emilia hissed at her sister. "Lower your voice immediately!"

"That girl is odd," Evelyn piped up. "She doesn't say anything!"

Emilia turned and glared at her nine-year-old sister.

"Many people would say you are odd because you say too much! Shame on you both! They are guests in our home and we treat them with the respect they deserve. What's more is you do not ever judge a someone for you do not know where they have come from!" Evelyn looked aghast, completely unaccustomed to being reprimanded by Emilia. Her own limpid eyes filled with tears.

"I didn't mean harm" she whispered. "I'm sorry, Emmy. I respect our guests!"

Emilia was filled with remorse as she watched her sister's face but she stood firm.

"When you respect people, you do not speak ill of them behind their backs. I want you to carefully consider your words before you speak from this day forward. You can cause someone a great deal of harm with your language and imagine how ashamed you will feel if that person needed a friend but instead were only met with idle name calling. You two are better than that! You were raised to be charitable and kind. Do not disappoint papa and I." Nodding, both girls shuffled upstairs to avoid any further punishment. As they disappeared, Abel walked into the kitchen.

"You will make a good mother," he told her quietly.

"Did you hear those two?" Emilia asked, placing a dish towel onto the counter, shaking her head in disbelief, purposely ignoring her father's comment. Abel nodded.

"Yes, I heard them. And I heard what you told them."

"Well it's true. They were raised better than that," Emilia said, reaching into the ice box for the cobbler she had made for dessert.

"I heard something else also," Abel said, drawing closer. Emilia glanced up.

"What else did you hear, father?" Abel gently touched her face so she was looking at him. He smiled genuinely, his eyes twinkling with happiness.

"I heard you call me 'papa.'"

Emilia had just finished hanging the wash on the line when she heard a faint knock at the door. Hurriedly, she picked up the basket and rushed inside. Unceremoniously, she threw open the door and her breath caught in her throat.

"Mr. Bawell!" He had been staring blankly into the yard and seemed to snap out of his reverie when Emilia spoke his name.

"Emilia," he nodded. He had a faraway look in his eye and he bit his lip as if in concentration.

"Are you all right?" Emilia questioned, trying to make sense of why he was standing on the doorstep. Unconsciously, her hand swept through her hair, smoothly the flyaway strands.

"No." Emilia stared expectantly at him, waiting for an elaboration which did not materialize. She sighed. He was still determined to be standoffish and she had far too much to do that day than vie for his affection.

"Mr. Bawell, my father is at the shop if you would like to speak with him," Emilia offered. Aaron blinked at her as if he did not comprehend her words.

"No," he said again, in a flat, monotonous way. "I need you."

Emilia's heart fluttered and she shushed it in her head but a smile could not help but find its way to her lips.

"Oh?" she asked with some uncharacteristic coyness. Her smile faded with his very next words.

"My daughter has vanished. I need you to help me find her."

## III

Night had fallen and there was still no trace of young Amity. Aaron Bawell sat perfectly still on a straight back chair, as if his soul had floated away from his body. A search party had formed and they had covered all of the hills and valleys in the district but no one had found a sign of the girl.

"She will turn up. She probably just got lost. They will find her," Abel told Aaron soothingly, trying to force his neighbor to eat and drink but Aaron was unhearing, unseeing and seemingly uncaring. The members of the community gathered in the bishop's home, waiting for word and speculating among themselves.

"Who would abduct a small Amish girl?" they wondered. "Our way is peaceful. This is unheard of!"

"She was not abducted," Emilia suddenly said, an epiphany hitting her full force. There was a murmur of skepticism as she began to pace excitedly, her mind racing.

"How can you know that, Emilia? This is commonplace with the English. Kidnapping and such. A stranger must have wandered off with her."

"No one wandered off with her," Emilia told them. "She has not been kidnapped."

"What do you believe happened to her?"

For the first time in hours, Aaron looked up, his once vacant eyes filled with hope.

"Where is my daughter, Emilia?" he begged, his voice hoarse with emotion.

"She went to where her mother is resting."

Amity had been walking for over seven hours, her little legs exhausted as she trekked toward her old district. It was Aaron himself who had found his small daughter, asleep on the side of the dirt road, completely hidden to eyes not searching. Her cheeks were caked in salted tears, her nose completely blocked from the endless crying her journey had seen. Aaron had flown off the carriage before it had come to a complete halt. He scooped up his daughter in strong arms and held her tightly but even that gesture did not wake the child from the depth of her sleep. Swaddling her like an infant, Aaron carefully placed her in the back of the wagon and sat with her as Abel took the reins and began the journey back to Latham District. Emilia sat in the wagon with father and daughter. Assured that Amity was still asleep, Aaron turned to the lovely blonde across from him. She could not make out his face as the wagon was dark and the night, moonless.

"How did you know?" he finally asked her. "How did you know where she had gone?"

Emilia was silent a moment. Ever since she had learned of Beth's death, it was as if a floodgate of memories had taken Emilia over. She began reliving every painful event which occurred from the moment her own mother had passed. When Aaron had arrived on the doorstep that afternoon, Emilia hadn't immediately made the connection but as time went on, it became clearer that Amity had not been taken and instead had run off somewhere. There was only one place the child wanted to be; with her mother. Of course Emilia knew that. That feeling was still very fresh in her own heart.

"I was Amity not too many years ago," Emilia told Aaron. "I understand how she feels."

There was a deep quiet from the other side of the transportation.

"I tried very hard," Aaron finally said.

"It is not easy," Emilia agreed.

"No. It is worse than that. Beth was sick for a great while. I had expected her to pass from when Amity was two years old. But she was a fighter, our Beth. She would get well and then get sick again, well and sick once more, each time getting worse and worse. Her body was failing. Everyone could see it including Beth. Our entire community knew it was only a matter of time. But Amity was just a baby. She only saw her mother. And she had so much hope that her mother would get well." Again, there was silence. Emilia opened her mouth to speak some words of comfort when Aaron took a breath.

"I despised my wife at the end of her life, Emilia. God help me, it's the truth. I loathed the fact that she would not give up and would continue to put our daughter through the trauma of watching her fall ill time and again. I am a despicable person. What kind of man wants his wife to die?" There was a catch in his voice and Emilia swallowed the lump in her own throat.

"The kind of man who cannot bear to watch others suffer," she answered quietly. "A very noble man. A man who loves his daughter so much that it tore him apart to watch her cry day after day for her mama." *A man like my father,* Emilia thought, her heart swelling with love for the man in the front of the carriage.

"I have been very uncouth to you, Emilia," Aaron suddenly said from the darkness. His voice was gruff.

"You have been grieving," she replied. "I do not consider a grieving man uncouth."

"No. That is not why I have been so uncivilized to you."

Emilia opened her mouth to protest but instead decided to wait for him to continue.

"When Beth found out she was dying, she made me promise to get married immediately so Amity would have a mother. She made numerous suggestions as to who should replace her. I agreed to placate her during her last days but the thought of marrying anyone else, of Amity calling anyone else 'mama' was horrifying and wrong. Some women in my community were overtly suggestive even prior to Beth's passing and when she finally did pass, there were knocks on my door quite literally the next day. That is why I made such a hasty decision to take Amity and leave."

"Ah, you thought I was one of the women vying for position of your wife," Emilia said slowly feeling her face blush crimson. *Oh papa! Do you see what your meddling has done now?*

"No, that's not what I believed, Emilia. I had seen you at church and you were so lovely, my breath actually halted when I laid eyes upon you. I had never felt that way about anyone. You are so beautiful but in a modest, unassuming form. I saw how well everyone has taken to you, how hard you work and how your sisters adore you. You are everything a man could hope for. I knew I had to stay far away from you. Yet when your father approached me in a neighborly fashion, I could not resist inviting you to supper. I wanted you near but I wanted you far away. Do you understand?"

Emilia almost laughed out loud.

"I understand exactly what you mean," she replied. "And now?"

Out of the dark, a large, calloused hand found hers. An unexpected shiver went up her spine at the touch. She squeezed his palm gently.

"And now the thought of marrying anyone other than you is horrifying and wrong." Aaron squeezed her hand back and for the first time since her mother died, Emilia felt the weight of the world lift off her shoulders.

She was actually happy.

END

# THE WEDDING DRESS

Chapter 1

Gabriela stared at her bank account, willing it to change. There was no way she was down to a hundred and twenty dollars. She wasn't getting paid for another three days! Even when she did get paid, a majority of it would get eaten up by her rent and groceries for that week. "Oh no," Gabriela said, laying her head on her arms. She didn't want to think about it, or look at it, or have anything to do with it. Unfortunately, when the problems are in your own life, you cannot exactly run away from them.

Gabriela wanted to call Bryan and get his support. She knew he would have all the verbal support she could want, but he wouldn't be able to loan her any money. His financial situation was just as bad as hers and he made even less money than she did. Once again, Gabby re-evaluated the idea of moving in with Bryan already. It would save them a few hundred bucks a month, and it wasn't so bad. After all, everyone was doing it.

"Maybe then, I would actually have money for a wedding dress," Gabby muttered to herself.

"Having a conversation with yourself again?" Reese asked her.

Gabby quickly minimized her bank account window. "Yes," she replied, trying to put aside her doubts to talk to her sister.

"You're starting to worry me. Turn that frown upside down!" Reese said, coming over and hugging Gabby.

Gabby couldn't help shaking her head and allowing a small smile to form on her lips. "Thanks, Reese." Reese started playing with Gabby's hair, brushing her fingers through its strands. Gabby closed her eyes and sunk into the sensation. It felt so calming to have her sister play with her hair as she had done since she was a little girl.

"Your graduation is in two weeks, isn't it?" Gabby asked, making slow conversation. Reese's hands felt so good.

"Yup! I can't believe I'm actually going to be done with high school. Then, I'm going to college, and that scholarship is seriously a blessing, don't you think?"

Gabby did her best at a nod. "Yes, I don't know how we would do it without that scholarship."

"Do you think Mom and Dad will come to my graduation?" Reese asked in a quiet voice. Gabby was glad she didn't have to look her sister full in the face as she answered.

"I don't know, Reese. Dad might not come because he thinks Mom will be there. Besides, he hasn't really been here for a while. I don't know. Mom might come."

"Do you think she'll bring her terrible boyfriend?"

"I don't know, Reese, but I want you to focus on your success, not on other people. You and only you have been the one responsible for getting yourself through high school. You have studied hard, and this is your time for a reward. I was thinking just you and me could go get ice cream at Scream Cream, maybe not that night but maybe the next if you are too busy partying."

Reese knew that Gabby's money situation was tight, but she just didn't know how tight. Gabby didn't dare let Reese in on the secret. They just needed to get through the summer then Reese would be in college, and Gabby would somehow pull together enough money for just a small wedding.

"When are you going to go dress shopping?" Reese asked after a few moments of silence.

"I don't know, Reese. I will be going soon. Don't worry. You will be invited."

"Yay! You know I am so excited for you! I'll still be able to come home for Thanksgiving or fall break to wherever you guys are, right?"

"Of course, Reese!" Gabby said, finally turning and looking her sister in the eye. "Come here." Even though Reese was eighteen, Gabby was still her big sister at twenty-five. "You will always be my baby," Gabby said, trying to make Reese sit on her lap.

"No!" Reese wailed. "I shall not! I am too old to be sitting on anyone's lap."

"Mmhmm," Gabby smiled mischievously. "I'll just tell that to your striking college boyfriend when you get him."

"Eww!" Reese said. "I'm not going to sit on anyone's lap."

Gabby laughed. "Sure, you say that now. Shall I videotape you saying it and show to you in five years? Come on, help me finish making that garlic bread."

Two days later, Gabby decided to pay a visit to Bryan. They wanted to have their wedding in the middle of August. At this point, they hadn't done anything more than decide it would be held on Bryan's family farm. That decision was based on the fact that it would be a free venue, including free flowers.

"Hey, Baby," Bryan said when Gabby dropped by at dinnertime. "I made something healthy for once. You should be proud of me."

Gabby laughed. "Of course, I'm proud of you. Reese and I rebelliously did not make a salad with our meal last night, so you are doing better than me."

"Come here," Bryan said, pulling her close. He gave her a sweet kiss. When he pulled back, Gabby smiled. This was why she was with him. He always made her feel at home. "Go ahead and sit down. I'll get you a drink in a minute," Bryan commanded.

Gabby took a seat and watched Bryan careen around the kitchen, pouring drinks, draining whole wheat pasta, and preparing their plates. When they finally sat down, Gabby took his hand and listened to Bryan pray. "Thank you, God, for this meal you have given us the resources to have. Please keep giving us all that we need. Amen."

The two began eating, and Gabby finally got up the nerve to bring up the old wedding topic. "Do you think we will even be ready to get married in August? That's only two and a half months away. I'm just worried that we won't have everything ready."

Bryan sighed, but Gabby knew that his frustration was not aimed at her. "I know it's stressful. But, we've almost gotten the rings paid for." Gabby realized at that moment that she forgotten to bring her ring payment that evening.

"Sorry!" Gabby interrupted. "I forgot my payment tonight. I'm getting paid tomorrow, though. I can just give you the money then, right?"

Bryan nodded. "That's fine. I know you're tight too. But, look, we'll have a beautiful meadow, rings, our pastor will come, and gorgeous wildflowers. Maybe we can ask guests to bring a dish. I know it's not conventional," Bryan said in response to Gabby's strange look. "But, maybe they will understand. Feeding so many people can be a few thousand dollars."

"I know," Gabby nodded. "And you paint a beautiful picture. I like the way it sounds. The problem is that. . .I really want to wear a special dress. I've always dreamed of a gorgeous white wedding dress, and I just don't know if I will be able to afford one. I don't want our wedding to just pass by like it's not anything special. I want to look beautiful for you." Gabby's voice cracked with emotion, and she looked down to avoid crying.

Bryan reached over and pat her hand. "I know that it is important to you. It's important to me that you have the wedding just how you want it. But I want you to know that whatever you choose to wear, I will love it." That was when Gabby realized that her yearning to wear such a beautiful gown might not be because she wanted Bryan to think she was beautiful. Maybe she just wanted to feel beautiful for once, not for anyone else but for herself.

Chapter 2

On Saturday, Gabby left Reese sleeping at home in bed to peruse the local flea market. She needed to get Reese a graduation present, but she also didn't have a lot of money to spend on something like that. She had no idea what she wanted to get her sister, but she knew that she liked to read. Perhaps, Gabby could find a few books at a reasonable price.

Gabby was looking at a table of books, holding a couple in her hands. The three books were only twelve dollars altogether, and Gabby thought they would be a great present for Reese right before her last free summer. Gabby looked up, and her eyes fell on a shining white dress hanging on a mannequin the next stall over. Gabby left the three books on the table and walked toward the dress as if in a trance.

Her hand reached up to stroke the fabric. Just as her fingers were going to touch the fabric, Gabby wondered if she should. She looked around to see if anyone was watching her. She saw a small, elderly woman with her eyes trained on her.

"Oh, sorry," Gabby said, stumbling into an apology. "I'm sorry. I didn't know if it was alright to touch, but it's so...pretty."

"Go ahead," the woman said in a raspy but friendly voice. "You may touch it." Her smile encouraged Gabby just the bit she needed to have the courage. She turned back to the dress and stroked it. It was soft, almost like silk. The beadwork was amazing, with little detail stitched along the folds of the fabric. The bosom was covered with exquisite beadwork, and the waist came in before flowing out in a long skirt. The train was not overwhelming but still had a presence. It was as though someone had created a wedding gown out of Gabby's imagination.

Gabby's breath caught in her throat. She didn't want to turn away from the beauty. She stealthily scanned the dress for a price tag. Of course, there was not one. That must mean that the dress was handmade and would cost even more.

"Th-thank you," Gabby said, turning away from the dress and nodding to the woman. She took a backward step away from the dress and the woman.

"Are you getting married?" the woman asked, leaning forward encouragingly.

"Yes," Gabby nodded. "But, we don't have a date yet. It will still be a few months." Finally, she shrugged her shoulders and figured she might as well ask how much the dress cost. If she didn't, she would constantly wonder. At least with a number, she could walk away from it without feeling guilty. "How much is the dress?" Gabby nodded toward the wedding dress she had been studying.

The old woman smiled and leaned back. "Oh, that dress doesn't have a price. I'm sure you noticed. It is a beautiful and priceless piece. But," the woman continued speaking before Gabby could turn away. "I will let you wear the gown for free if you promise me one thing."

"What?" Gabby whispered, unable to wait to hear her words.

"You must live out your marriage according to God's will."

"I-uh-oh," Gabby seemed unwilling to respond. "I can wear it. . .for free?"

The woman nodded. "There's a veil that goes with the dress as well, but I must have you promise that your marriage will be uplifting to God. Can you do that?"

"I promise with my whole heart," Gabby said. She couldn't control the smile that spread across her face.

The woman nodded. "Very well. God, our good Lord, will hold you to your word. Now, just give me a moment to gather the dress and package it safely. Do you have a few minutes?"

"Yes, of course!" Gabby could hardly believe her good fortune. "Do you need any help? I could help you."

"That blue bag up there on the shelf, yes, that one. That's the veil. Go ahead and get that down, will you?" Gabby strained up to reach the high shelf, took down the bag, and could not help peering into the bag to examine the veil.

"What do you think?" the woman asked, nodding at the veil.

"It's amazing," Gabby said. The woman carefully took out the veil and used the comb part to place the veil on Gabby's head. She handed Gabby a small hand-mirror, and Gabby nearly cried. She looked like a real bride, not a bride who didn't have any money. Spontaneously, Gabby reached down and hugged the old woman. "Thank you," she sobbed out. The woman patted Gabby's back.

Finally, Gabby carefully folded the veil and put it back in the bag. She then helped the woman take the dress off the mannequin and store it in a garment bag.

"I have one more thing for you," the woman said as Gabby prepared to leave. The woman pulled out a thick book. "I want you to take a look at this. This dress, you see, has a long history. It has made many brides happy on their wedding day, and they all needed it in one way or another. I encourage you to find out about their stories and write your own as well."

Gabby took the thick, leather bound book in the crook of her arm and tried to give the woman one last hug while balancing her packages. "How will I find you again?" Gabby asked.

"I'm always right here," the woman assured her. "Come back after your wedding, and I'll be waiting."

Gabby smiled, thanked the woman one more time, then hurried out of the flea market, forgetting all about Reese's graduation present. The smile could not be wiped off her face. She carefully laid the dress across her backseat and could not help but sing along with every song on the radio. The only thing left to do was try it on. When she reached home, she carried the dress inside and explained the whole story to Reese who at first felt deceived that her sister had gone wedding dress shopping without her.

"I'm going to try it on," Gabby said. "Wait until I'm in it, okay? Don't come in!" Gabby shut the door with her sister outside and changed as carefully as she could into the wedding dress. Gabby could tell the dress had had sleeves at some point. But, it was now a sleeveless dress. The hem was a little long, but Gabby knew she could fix that. Around her waist, the dress fit perfectly. Gabby tucked the veil into place then opened the door with a smile.

"Sis!" Reese said. The smile filling her face was all that Gabby needed to see. "It's perfect isn't it?"

"Yes, it is!" Reese gave Gabby a hug. "I can't believe you are actually getting married!"

"It seems real now."

"It is real," Reese said. "I know Bryan would love you in this dress. I wish he could see it now."

"I know!" Gabby laughed. "But it has to be our secret. "No words to him about it. None, do you hear me?"

Later that night, Bryan came over. He got along well with Reese, and Gabby loved that about him. After all, she might not be Reese's official guardian, but she was Reese's home ever since their parents had started their incessant bickering.

The three were playing a game of Phase 10, and Reese kept smiling randomly at Gabby. "Is something wrong with you?" Bryan asked her. "Or do you two have a cheat going on?"

Both Gabby and Reese laughed. "Nope, we're not cheating," they said in unison.

"Okay, because that denial was totally believable. Come on, I know something is up." Gabby looked at Reese. They both shrugged, but Gabby could not longer keep the news in.

"I got my wedding dress today," Gabby said.

"What?! That's amazing, Gabby. Where is it? Can I see it? Was it expensive?"

"To all of those questions, the answer is no. Besides, the groom is never supposed to see the dress before the wedding day."

"I've got an idea," Bryan said, leaning forward. "Want to get married tomorrow?"

"Sorry," Gabby shook her head. "Pastor is occupied tomorrow. Besides, I'm not ready yet."

"Aw," Bryan visibly drooped. "I guess we should probably wait until we have rings, huh?"

"That would be important!" Gabby said. She gave Bryan a playful kiss and was glad that she did not feel as desperate for a dress as she had that morning.

Chapter 3

Gabby carefully opened the book the woman had given her the day before. In the excitement of trying on the dress and spending time with Bryan, she hadn't thought about it again until she and her sister were leaving church. She hadn't told her sister about the book or how exactly she had gotten the dress, but she had told her enough to be satisfied.

The book appeared to be some sort of journal. On the pages were handwritten notes, some in cursive, some printed, and clearly not all done by the same person. Beside each handwritten note was a picture of a woman wearing the wedding dress. Gabby ran her hands over the first picture. The dress had had sleeves, just as Gabby suspected. The picture looked old, and it was worn around the edges. But it had stayed faithfully in the book. Beside it was a note.

"Teresa Daniels, age twenty-four. Married to Bertram Frantz, age twenty-four, on May 7, 1978. My parents had both died when I was five. I had been living with a family friend since then. The boy I grew up living next to asked me to marry him, but I didn't have any money for a wedding, let alone a beautiful dress. I met this wonderful young woman who loaned me a dress that she had just finished making. She told me to tell my story and live my marriage in a way that would make God pleased with me. I am determined to do just that. My adoptive parents may not have enough money to pay for a wedding, but this wedding dress shows just how much God is looking out for us."

Underneath the note was Teresa Frantz's contact information. In different handwriting was a little note that said she had died in a car accident in 2004. Gabby suddenly felt as though she was holding something very sacred. The dress was only used perhaps once a year, if that, and Gabby hungrily read through each story. Each woman had something to say about how she did not have enough money or something had befallen her. Gabby wondered why their contact information was there. Did they really want someone to talk to them? And what did they want to talk about?

Gabby pictured herself eight years from now with a few small children. She would always remember how she had gotten her wedding dress. What would she say to someone else who was going to use it? Gabby could only smile.

She selected two of the most recent weddings and decided to write to their email addresses. Her message was simple.

"Hi, my name is Gabriela. I'm going to use the wedding dress. I found your information in the book, and I was wondering if you'd like to meet and have a coffee."

Gabriela went to bed at close to two in the morning. "I am so not going to be awake for work in the morning," Gabby said. She had received her payment in her account over the weekend, and Gabby spent a little time that Monday morning paying her bills. It was just as nasty as ever. Even though she had a wedding dress now, she still would not be able to save any money after paying everything necessary. She sighed and shook her head. "It's okay," she told herself.

The workday passed well enough, but Reese was celebrating when she got home because she only had two more exams before she was officially done with school. Gabby spent some of the evening quizzing Reese before she gave herself the luxury of checking her email. She had received a reply.

"It's nice to hear from you, Gabriela. I would love to meet for coffee. How does Wednesday at lunch hour sound? Would it be possible for me to meet you at the Starbucks in Clayton?

Annabel"

Gabriela rejoiced over the email. She couldn't wait to meet this woman and unravel a bit more of the dress mystery.

When it finally came time for her Wednesday lunch hour, Gabby drove as quickly as she could to the Starbucks. She ordered and looked around for Annabel. She finally found her, and the two shook hands in a formal manner.

"I'm so glad you reached out and contacted me," Annabel said. "I wondered if anyone ever would."

Gabby smiled excitedly. "I can't believe the dress was first loaned out in 1978. It still looks so new."

"Well," Annabel surmised. "The sleeves were taken off, and I think some extra beadwork was added."

"Still," Gabby smiled. "It's like I'm wearing a little bit of history."

Annabel laughed. "Yeah, it's magical the way that woman wants to help us. It's like she can just sense the desperation in someone."

"So, what's your story?" Gabby asked, wanting to fill in the blanks Annabel's note had left.

Annabel nodded. "I was eighteen when I got the wedding dress. I know, I was young. I didn't want to get married yet, but my boyfriend had gotten me pregnant. I had just found out a few days before. I had talked to my boyfriend, and he and I decided we would just have a quiet wedding, a justice of the peace deal. I didn't want to do that, but I knew we needed to do something quickly. I didn't want to be one of those boldly pregnant brides. But I was so frustrated with the whole situation, that I had just decided I would wear an old dress. It didn't matter.

"When I saw that wedding dress, though, I couldn't help but be drawn to it. When the woman told me it was free for my use as long as I lived a godly marriage, I couldn't believe my good fortune. We had a justice of the peace wedding, but I was wearing a gorgeously beautiful wedding gown. I will never forget that woman's generosity." Annabel shook her head.

"So, it made your day magical?" Gabriela asked in excitement.

Annabel laughed aloud. "Yes, it sure did. My wedding may not have been what I had imagined it to be when I was fifteen or sixteen, but it was much better than it would have been under the circumstances. Now, I have Gracen, and she's getting close to her second birthday."

"Wow! That's so amazing."

"What's your story?" Annabel leaned forward and listened as Gabriela told her about her all the financial troubles she had had. Gabriela and Annabel continued chatting until the last possible minute.

"I really need to get back to my job," Gabby said, "Or I could lose it. That is definitely not what I need right now. Look, I really enjoyed talking to you. Maybe we could get together again, and I could meet Gracen?"

"I'd like that," Annabel said. "I'll talk to you later."

Chapter 4

Gabriela finally got a reply from the other woman she had contacted about meeting: Brianne. Brianne's story had seemed really tragic, and Gabriela couldn't wait to hear about it from the woman's lips.

After the introductions, Gabriela leaned forward for Brianne's story. "I'm really glad you wanted to talk," Brianne said. "I feel like this dress has created a secret group."

"Have you ever talked to Annabel?" Gabriela asked.

"Annabel. . .Annabel. I don't think so. Was she married after me?"

"I don't remember," Gabriela said. "But I have her number. Maybe we could all three get together or even more brides."

Brianne smiled. "I like the idea. I am definitely willing to contribute. Okay, so here's what happened to me. My problem was not so much a financial one as I read in so many stories. Instead, my problem was a big fire. About five days before the date our wedding was set, some sort of electrical malfunction sparked in our house. My family lost everything. Insurance took care of the problem financially, but the dress I had so carefully picked out months before along with my shoes and veil had been consumed by the fire. Trying to get a dress five days before a wedding is pretty much impossible.

"But, this beautiful old lady performed a miracle. She let me borrow the dress. It was much better than the dress I had originally picked. Better than that, it was ready for the wedding two days early." Brianne shook her head. "I had thought I might need to call off the wedding. I was freaking out. I couldn't even go to work I was so stressed out. I had a few burn marks from escaping the house, but the dress covered them nicely. They can't even be seen in the photos."

"Wow!" Gabby said, soaking in her new friend's story. "Wow." She was silent for a few minutes as Brianne's story sunk in. "Did you know that there have been thirty-three weddings in that dress? I'll be number thirty-four."

"When is your wedding?" Brianne asked.

"It'll be mid-August, right after my sister moves into her college dorm. She's been living with me."

"Would you mind if I rudely invited myself to your wedding?" Brianne smiled.

Gabby laughed. "Of course not. You are welcome. It's going to be a small wedding, and we ask that each guest bring a dish of food, a sort of potluck. We really don't have the money for much more, but I would be honored for you to come."

After meeting the two brides, Gabby wanted to meet more. She kept setting up even more appointments with brides. She had one last meeting planned before her wedding. This meeting took a few weeks to set up. By the time Gabby met her, it was the first day of August.

"What's your story?" Gabby asked impatiently. The question had become one of which she could not wait to ask each new woman. Hallie had been married almost ten years ago.

"My story's probably a bit different from some others," Hallie shook her head. Gabby had agreed to come to her house because Hallie had three young children. Hallie wanted them to be able to play and stay out of their hair while the two women talked. "I was poor. I couldn't buy a wedding dress. That much is as normal as for any of us women."

Gabby nodded, anticipating more.

"My story becomes interesting after I married Mark. Did the lady have you make a promise?"

Gabby nodded. "Yes, I promised that I would live my marriage according to God's will."

Hallie accepted Gabby's words. "Yes, I promised the same thing. At the time, I promised it because it seemed such an easy exchange for the dress. But it wasn't as easy as I thought it would be. The first year of marriage was so difficult. I looked back on the innocence I sported on my wedding day, and I would shake my head. How had I thought I loved Mark?" Hallie was quiet as she remembered. "I was sure that we were going to get a divorce. You see, his family lives on the other side of the country. I know he was really close to them, but he agreed that living here would be the best solution for us.

"But, it was like he had forgotten that. We argued almost every night. I started to hate him. He made me cry so much." Hallie shook her head, and Gabby should see the tears brimming in her eyes. "I started fantasizing about running away and going a place where he wouldn't find me. Then, I remembered my promise. I tried to weasel my way out of it, saying that the fighting was Mark's fault. I blamed him, but I knew I needed to take credit for my part. So, I started serving Mark instead of myself.

"Even when I was tired, I would make dinner. I would clean up without complaint. He noticed after a month, and I felt him become more tender toward me. We were finally able to talk through what had been happening. That was the best day of my life, the day that we finally talked it all through without screaming. I finally slept next to him and felt connected to him again.

"Gabby, that promise is going to be hard to keep. You will probably get angry with your fiance sometimes, but don't walk away. The weak walk away; it's the strong that keep fighting."

Gabby hugged Hallie as a few tears spilled over. "Thank you, Hallie. I needed to hear those words. They were just what I needed." Before Gabby left Hallie's house, she invited her to her wedding. "I know it is only two weeks, but if you think you can come, I would really like it. Don't be shy about bringing your husband and children."

Chapter 5

On the day of her wedding, Gabby carefully donned the dress. It was to be a simple ceremony. Only her sister would stand beside her. Bryan was having his best friend stand beside him. At that moment nothing felt simple about Gabby as she waited for Reese to calmly do up the back.

"I can't believe it's really the day," Gabby said.

Reese smiled. "Yeah, I'm pretty sure I'm having the most exciting first weekend home from college out of all of my friends." Of course, her statement made Gabby start asking about all of Reese's new friends. She had to make sure that her baby sister was doing well and having fun in college.

"Is it done?" Gabby asked.

Reese nodded. "It's done. You're all ready."

"Well, not completely," Gabby said. "I look fine, but I feel a bit nervous about walking down that aisle."

"Why?" Reese asked. "Are you unsure about Bryan?"

"No," Gabby shook her head. "I know he is perfect for me, well, as perfect a fit as someone can be with my rather strange personality."

Reese laughed. "Then, what is making you nervous?"

"I guess it just hit me that this is a lifelong commitment. I love Bryan, and I just don't want anything to go wrong. What if we start living together, and he does annoying things that get on my nerves?"

"Like what?"

"Like leave his socks on the bed."

"Then tell him to take his socks off," Reese shrugged. "It's not that hard. Look, if you love him and you know that for sure, then you just have to go through the bad stuff and remember that. Then you'll get to the good times, and it'll be all worth it."

"Alright, my sister the wise," Gabby smiled. "What time is it?"

Reese looked at her phone. "We still have thirty minutes."

"What a long thirty minutes that'll be!" Gabby sighed, carefully sitting in her dress.

Reese laughed aloud. "I thought you just said you were nervous to do it, and now you can't wait to go down the aisle."

Gabriela laughed with her sister. "When you get to this point, I will be right by your side and remind you of everything you just said. Meanwhile, you'll just be like. No, I'm nervous! Let me be nervous by myself!"

Gabriela's friend Erica burst into the bedroom just then. "Hey! Wow, Gabby! You look so amazing!" Erica was the unofficial photographer. She had a professional camera and had done some photo shoots. A free photographer was her wedding gift to her friend. "Look, we don't have a lot of time, but I wanted to get a few pictures of just you in all your bridal beauty, then maybe a few with Reese. Hey, Reese! How are you?" Erica said in one breath.

Gabby laughed. "Oh, Erica, I knew there was a good reason we were friends." Erica took all the photos she wanted with Gabby sitting, standing, lounging, smiling, and serious.

"Alright, Reese, get in there with your sister." After a few more shots, Erica hovered over to the door. "Alright, I believe we have five minutes before your little flower girl will start her march. Let's get you safely down these stairs."

Gabby carefully maneuvered the stairs with the help of her sister and friend. The stairs were not very wide and definitely not prepared to have brides tramping up and down them. She finally stood by the back doors.

"Ready?" Reese asked.

Because Gabby had decided against having their estranged father walking her down the aisle, Reese would be walking right beside her.

"I think so," Gabby answered. "But ask me again in a minute, and I might have a different answer."

"You've got this, Sis."

"Thanks."

Erica reappeared as the music started to assist the flower girl on her way. Next went the ringbearer. After that came Gabby and Reese. It was a simple, small wedding, just as Gabby had dreamed it. Best of all was Bryan's face when she came through the doors of the back of the farmhouse.

His smile was genuine and delighted, and Gabby looked only at him as Reese guided her steps down the aisle. When she reached the altar, she placed her hands in Bryan's, smiling into his eyes and wondering how she had ever doubted her decision to marry him.

"I love you," she whispered as the pastor was talking to them. He mouthed the words back and gave her hands a squeeze. Suddenly, the ceremony, including a candle lighting, a song sung by a friend, and a short talk from the pastor seemed all too long to Gabby. After what seemed an eternity, the words she had wanted to hear for so long pierced her thoughts.

"You may now kiss the bride."

Gabby kissed Bryan, leaning into his lips. When they pulled back, Gabby felt the magic of the moment lingering. "You're my husband," she whispered, incredulous.

"And you, my dear, are my wife." Bryan let go of one of her hands, facing the audience. The pastor announced them, and Bryan paused before they started down the aisle. "This is my wife!" he shouted, his pleasure clear as he lifted up their joined hands in victory. Gabby started laughing. Suddenly, a huge cheer rose up from the back of the rows of seats. Gabby looked over and counted five of the former brides that she had met.

"Yes, Gabriela!" They screamed together. While Gabby had not pictured her wedding as loud as a ballgame, she couldn't help laughing aloud.

Bryan carefully led her down the steps, and they entered the old farmhouse. As soon as they were inside, Bryan turned to her and kissed her passionately. "You are the most beautiful bride I have ever seen," he whispered. "And tonight, I will make you mine." Gabby trembled with anticipation, leaning in for another kiss.

A week later, Gabby carefully zipped the wedding dress into the garment bag for the last time. She took out the book and carefully glued in a photo of herself wearing the dress. She smiled at the photo then took up a pen and began writing in her best cursive beside the photo.

"Gabriela Winfox, age twenty-five. Married to Bryan Davis on August 21, 2016. This dress changed my life. Not only did it give me a chance to have the kind of wedding I would never have had on my budget, but it showed me the friendliness and generosity this kind of world doesn't see very often. It made me promise to be a more generous person and to look for opportunities to help others. I didn't have any money for a nice wedding, and my fiance and I feared we would not be able to throw a wedding. Determined to get married, because we knew it was right, I thought I would never have a wedding dress. I was wrong. Please, contact me. I would love to talk to you, and I know that the brides I met would love to talk to you as well. We are in this together."

*Gabriela signed her name under her words and closed the book with a solemn thud. "Thank you, God," she said as she loaded the dress, veil, and book into the back of her car. She was on her way to the flea market.*

# AMANDA ROBERS

**Chapter 1: Just an Amish Girl**

Naomi Zook never took pleasure in extravagant things. Her name Naomi, however, did literally mean, pleasant. Even when she became of age to experience Rumspringa, the time in which Amish girls and boys are allowed to experience the outside world, she did not find joy in living life outside of her quiet Amish community. She was a simple Amish girl through and through. She was also incredibly shy. Anyone who ever met or associated with Naomi would have few things to say about her, good, bad, or otherwise. She came from the Zook family; they lived a more or less traditional Amish-style life... no electricity, no cars, no cell phones. Her father was a woodworker and her mother was a quiltmaker. Naomi took on her mother's trade of quilt-making, in addition to making Amish-style dolls, and knitted slippers. Their family's lifestyle was certainly a humble way of life and nobody would dare say anything different. Even among the other Amish families in the community, no one had a bad thing to say about the Zooks.

Naomi, 18, spent her days split between assisting at the one-room schoolhouse, making quilts, sewing dolls, milking the family cow, and feeding the chickens. Naomi's family didn't own a whole farm like some families, but they had one cow for a milk and a dozen chickens for eggs. Naomi didn't love making quilts for her mother's business, but you would never know because not a single complaint ever escaped between her lips in front of the others. Naomi's mother, Rebekah Zook, was even more conservative that Naomi, and believed that Naomi existed simply to serve her. Naomi, being the only girl of six children, found herself doing a significant amount of the housework as well as sewing.

Being not only the only girl, but also the oldest, she was a very mature young lady, who wanted to not just sew her brother's torn clothes, but also, she desired to sew overalls for her future husband, whoever he was. She didn't find anything interesting about the "English boys," their cigarettes, their booze, or their addiction to their thumbs.

She didn't understand what was so interesting about a bunch of colored candies in a row. What exactly was so fascinating on the phone that kept them from missing out on real life? None of them knew how to watch a sunset, to sit quietly without speaking or playing on their phones, or enjoy the tranquility of an evening fire.

She didn't understand why some of her girlfriends grew up and chose to leave the Amish community. She did understand, however, that some things, none of the girls liked, not even her. Being a woman in an Amish community, meant you needed to do almost everything. But in fact, Naomi didn't mind doing everything, but what she did want was a supportive husband by her side. Someone who would help her maintain a few animals, maintain some income for the house, and eat her cooking experiments in the kitchen.

Of the few things that she enjoyed from Rumspringa was some of the "modern" ingredients that she could use in baking and cooking. How easy it was to make a cake with premade icing (not that she didn't mind making her own icing.) How easy it was to buy a large tub of butter, rather than to make her own! Easy come easy go. Sometimes she worried about how she loved some of the conveniences of the outside world, but still, she was Amish through and through. Naomi even found a love of African pottery. She experienced the arts during her time away from the community, saw art museums, bought unique art supplies with her limited savings from selling Amish dolls, and even took an African pottery class.

Whenever Naomi expressed a desire for anything other than quilt-making, working hard for the family, feeding the chicken, milking the cow or cooking dinner, Naomi's mother would sigh with disgust. Although she didn't say anything, she didn't have to. One look from her mother and she would certainly not utter a word about wanting pottery supplies. For certain, her mother would remind her immediately that she chose to remain Amish. Her mother said almost every day with her face "Thank God that she will not bring shame to her family with interests in silly things such as African pottery and boxed cake mixes! Good Lord save us all."

**Chapter 2: Traded Goods**

One day, on Naomi's route to deliver quilts, dolls, slippers, and other sewn and knitted goods, she was surprised to find herself blushing at the door of the Kings' house when a young man called Amos answered the door. She had seen Amos at church meetings, barn-raisings, and the like, but she never had a conversation with him. She usually did not have a delivery from the King's home for any sewn goods, because their grandmother was, of course, also a homemaker, and used to make quilts herself. These days, however, their grandmother had been very sick in bed, due to a genetic disease called Cystic Fibrosis, that seemed to take over the poor woman's body. Although it was hardly uncommon for some diseases to crop up inside families, there was little the Kings' could do for their grandmother except to keep her comfortable.

They couldn't do much for her simply because of the nature of the disease; it certainly wasn't due to a lack of monetary resources, as they had a very nice-sized farm. The King's farm employed many children of families in the village who did not have their own farm. They were also always generous with what they had. Their names seemed to fit their finances, but they were among the humblest of families in the community. They were not only Kings on Earth, but they would be kings in Heaven too. Namoi was sure of that. Naomi's mother, Rebekah, never spoke about the King family but then again, she never spoke about any family other than her own.

When Amos opened the door to their home to accept the quilt a small toothy smile crossed his face. Naomi was surprised to see Amos smiling at her, as he had never paid her any attention before in the community. When she thought about it, she never really noticed him either, but here she was standing in front of his door. Amos begins speaking with her and asked her to come inside while he obtained payment for the quilt that his grandmother ordered. His grandmother used to be one of the best quiltmakers, but she wanted one from Rebekah because she knew the quality of her work. Amos asked Naomi to come inside and have a glass of lemonade. It was not polite to leave the young lady standing on her doorstep after all. As Naomi came inside she immediately noticed that everything was in order. Everything had its place. Nothing was overdone or too exquisite. The only thing that revealed the Kings' families' wealth, besides the farm, of course, was the solitary grandfather clock that stood in the corner. Amos caught Naomi staring at the grandfather clock, and slightly embarrassed explained that it was a family heirloom. Amos didn't want Naomi to think that they were extravagant people. He knew that her family members were simply people, much like his.

Naomi was trying her hardest to listen to Amos' words about the grandfather clock but couldn't help but notice the beauty of his face. Everything from his black hat that every unmarried boy wore, to the sharp high edges of his cheekbones made her smile. He had slightly worn skin and calluses on his hands from working on the farm, but there was color in his cheeks and a bounce in his step. His hair was a light brown color, and his eyes were a precious dark brown. She found herself getting lost in his eyes and his high cheekbones and almost forgot that Amos was speaking. Amos paused and asked her if she didn't like her lemonade because she wasn't drinking it. She had almost forgotten entirely about her lemonade due to fact that she was gazing at Amos. Slightly embarrassed she drank her lemonade quickly. Amos offered another glass of homemade lemonade, and she shook her head saying she had to get back to her mother's house. Immediately. He then offered a silver of shoe-fly pie, but Naomi couldn't deny a well-made slice of shoe-fly pie. After all, who could turn down shoe-fly pie? Amos gave her payment in the form of more food than was necessary. He loaded her sack with cucumbers, tomatoes, fresh bread, home-made cheeses, a gallon of chicken corn soup, a bottle of home-made wine, and a jar of home-made peanut butter. Naomi tried to refuse at least the bottle of wine, but Amos insisted.

As she turned to go, he asked her to wait. Oh, Naomi, if you don't mind can you please make a few dolls for my young cousins. When you bring them, I'll certainly have a few more jars of home-made peanut butter ready for you. Amos' smile spread across his face like the stars lighting up the night sky on a clear night.

**Chapter 3: How Could It Feel Like This?**

A few days later, Naomi found herself bumping into Amos almost everywhere she went. How could it be that no matter where she was, Amos was there? After church on Sunday, Amos stayed for singing and was seated only a few seats away from her. She was wishing that he would ask to take her home or ask her out on a date, but nothing of the sort happened. After the singing, the youth were mixing, chatting, and talking as usual. Finally, Amos approached and made small talk. "How is your mother?" he asked Naomi. "Oh, fine, thank you, you know busy making quilts of course. She really truly loved your peanut butter, and she would never admit it, but she loved the wine too!" Naomi replied.

Amos laughed, and Naomi could almost feel his laugh reverberate through her soul. Naomi thought to herself that maybe she could even marry Amos. How could it be that without even touching his hand or passing more than a few minutes together she could feel like this? Amos' smile crept across his face because he wanted very much to ask Naomi to go out with him. He knew very well that Naomi had already turned down the opportunity to leave the Amish community, and so did he. He was not interested in what the outside world had to offer. Although he enjoyed some small pleasures of the outside world, he did not find that it was necessary to leave his family and his home just to have a simpler or easier life. It took him less than 24 hours to get used to the idea of flipping a switch and having electricity, lights, and a hot oven. Regardless of these conveniences, he never for a moment wanted to give up his Amish upbringing, family, values, and culture. Now he was even more certain of his decision as he saw something in Naomi that warmed his heart. What he would now, he just wasn't sure, but he would leave that thought process for another day.

The two found themselves with an awkward pause in the conversation as they realized that everyone had stopped speaking except for the two of them. Naomi suddenly bid him good night so as not to draw too much more attention to their conversation or time spent together. Naomi leaned in to give Amos an awkward half-hug that clearly wanted to be something more. She leaned in with one arm and pulled Amos into a tight hug that Amos returned half-heartedly. Actually, Amos wanted to give her a full-on frontal hug with both arms and kiss her forehead, but instead, he embraced her quickly and said good night.

Naomi quickly noticed that everyone was looking, and so she walked way in a hurried fashion. She met her mother outside the door of the church gathering. Immediately her mother had questions "Who was that boy you were hugging?" "The son of Faith King, no?" The questions and comments continued, "He's a good boy, you know, but you have no business starting anything with any boy. Naomi, you know very well that we need you here at the house. With all your brothers to feed and the house to clean, Naomi, you mustn't think about boys for a good long while..." her mother stated quite bluntly. That was it. Immediately the end of that conversation. "How was your friend, Ruth, darling?" asked Naomi's mother. "Oh, fine, yeah she's working on the farm, of course." "Like, a good Amish daughter, very, very good," replied Naomi's mother.

**Chapter 4: The Usual Rhythm**

A few weeks passed since Naomi had seen Amos. Rebekah had hoped that her daughter had forgotten entirely about this boy nonsense, but, in fact, quite the opposite was occurring for Naomi. The more time she stayed without seeing Amos, the more she daydreamed about marrying Amos, having her own family, having her first baby, making her own home, and maybe even making pottery too! Needless to say, she kept all those thoughts quiet to herself. After all, there were things that needed to be attended to at the house as usual.

Naomi continued her days, more or less, as usual. From 4 am to 6 am she was up bright and early, to tend the family cow and the few chickens. She fed the animals, collected any eggs, cleaned the trough, and refilled the water bowl for the chickens. Around 6 am she drank some warm milk and fried some doughnuts for everyone to eat for breakfast. The days passed like this in a very predictable pattern. After breakfast, there were house chores, cleaning the bathroom, washing the dishes, and inevitably, in the afternoon hours when it was simply too hot to be outside, Naomi sat wither mother in the parlor making quilts together. Plus, three days a week Naomi helped with teaching at the school.

There was only the sound of knitting needles clicking against each other, and the occasional comment from her mother about her progress on the quilts, until her brothers came home from school in the mid-afternoon hours. Naomi's mind stirred to one thing as it drew near the weekend. There was a barn-raising this weekend and she was bound to see Amos at the barn-raising. Everyone in the community always attended a barn-raising. It was coming to the end of the summer and fall was trying ever so hard to make its appearance. The leaves on the trees were still all green, but she could almost feel fall in the crisp fresh air of the countryside.

One of the things that she loved about her life was that the air was always fresh. In addition, fall was her favorite season. The air was also fresh with the smell of the animals sometimes, especially in the planting season, but she didn't mind that at all in comparison to the pollution, the cigarette smoke, and the nonsense that occurred in the city. Soon, the leaves would change colors, from greens to vibrant yellows, bright oranges, and raging reds. As a child, she loved to make leaf piles and jump in them. She always thought that she was just like every other child until she went on Rumspringa. Then she knew, she wasn't like all the other children. She actually liked her lifestyle better. Her life was not intruded upon by the outside culture of the others, their technology, and constant addiction to their phones. She could not accept how much the youth her own age were tip-tap-tapping away on their iPhones and i-whatevers.

Her mind wandered back to the upcoming barn-raising. The barn simply had to go up before the first frost. A newly married couple were starting their own small farm, and the community wanted to support the new family unit. She always loved barn-raisings. They naturally were a lot of work for everyone, and the women spent all day cooking, catering to the men, and bringing food and water to them, but she was always impressed by their ability to build a barn in one day. It's amazing what the whole community does when it comes together.

## Chapter 5: Barn-Raising Day

Finally, the day of the barn-raising arrived. It was a beautiful early Saturday morning and the sun was not quite able to make an appearance yet when Amos got out of bed and donned his denim overalls and workmen's boots. Amos loved barn-raising days. He loved his family's farm too, but what he loved more was construction. Any task or project that allowed him to get his hands dirty literally, he loved, especially construction. Building something, feeling a part of something, feeling a part of a structure that would make his community stronger was more important than almost anything to him, except, God and his family. Recently though his mind seemed to wander to Naomi. She was a smart young lady, smart enough to understand the value of family and hard-work, and was, well, quite attractive too. After all, how could he not notice? Perhaps she liked him too? Did he like her? Her soft brown curls wrapped around her face, as soft as a peach from his mother's garden. He barely felt her cheeks graze his face when she went in to give him a hug at the church singing. He wasn't quite ready to admit that he had feelings for her, but after all, eventually, he wanted to marry a nice girl and start his own life. Amos pushed the thoughts of Naomi out of his head as he got ready to head to the location of the barn-raising with his father, mother, brothers, and sisters. Being one of 10 meant that there was always work to do, but it also always meant that there was an extra set of hands ready. Amos always loved being a part of a big family. He loved the feeling of being surrounded by those who love him in a home filled with laughter, singing, and even the smell of fresh bread and homemade wines. What more could you ask from life?

As Amos, his family, and the entire town gathered at the site of the barn-raising, Amos caught himself scanning the horizon for Naomi. How silly of me, he thought. Why am I looking for Naomi on the day of the barn-raising? The men and boys gathered, as the oldest and most experienced engineer in the community gave instructions and assigned tasks according to the skill level of each worker. Boys were to handle cutting and passing the plywood to the young men who assisted the leads of each group who were setting the foundation for the barn. The foundation was the hardest part. Once the foundation was finished there was no need to worry about the rest. The rest of the barn almost seemed to complete itself with the number of hands they had on deck.

Naomi found herself occupied through maintaining the food tables, arranging fruits, vegetables, cheeses, bread, and even hamburgers and hot dogs. On special days, they feasted even with "English food." Who didn't like a good hamburger, right? She kept her mind occupied with the festivities and enjoyed the fact that she was assigned to such a large task. Actually, it wasn't a very large task in comparison with building a barn, but still, she was always given more responsibilities than some of the other girls who never took a barn-raising seriously. They thought of it as a way to get escape responsibilities for the day and hide somewhere in the shade flirting with a boy who also found it more important to flirt than to prepare lumber.

As the day passed, the hungry team of workers assembled in the line, and orchestrated the food line. She had it down to a science. There was space for people to pass on both sides of the tables quickly, and as they filled their plates and stomachs, she refilled the baskets of food. Just as the basket of fresh rolls was looking empty, she looked up to find Amos reaching for a roll. He locked eyes with her, and startled said," Oh, hi Naomi, sorry, I didn't see you there." "Hi Amos, how are you doing today?" replied Naomi. "Great, thanks, you know, I love barn-raising days, then again, most of us do." Answered Amos. "Sure, of course," Naomi replied. Amos caught Naomi off-guard and said, "You look awfully nice today," "Oh, it's just the same thing I wear every day, but I am excited about seeing the new barn." replied Naomi.

The two laughed. "That must be it then," said Amos. Growing more self-conscious of the line going around them, Naomi suddenly remembered the basket of rolls. "Hey Naomi, are you going to refill the rolls or do I have to do it?" shouted Rebekah, Naomi's mother. "Mom, I was just..." and then Naomi was interrupted. "You were just, what?" asked her mother. "Nothing," said Naomi. When Naomi looked up Amos was gone. Certainly, he had to eat of course, but why did her mother look up at exactly the same time when she had finally spotted Amos?

## Chapter 6: Trouble Lurking

Meanwhile in the corner of the room stood, Linda Stoltzfus, one of the busy bodies of the community. Everybody knew who the busybodies were, but nobody cared. Nobody took them seriously, but Linda on that day wanted to be taken seriously. Had she just seen Amos flirting with Naomi? Or was it Naomi flirting with Amos? No, that can't be. Naomi was such a plain boring girl, just doing whatever her mother asked or wanted. She was a few years younger than Naomi but she had her eye on Amos for quite some time. She certainly was not going to let some nose-wiping girl like Naomi snatch Amos out from her under her feet, now was she? Well, she would see about that. Amos, after all, was a catch. Almost every girl pined after Amos, his dark brown eyes, his rough, strong hands, and of course his family had a delightfully large farm and income. His family was well-to-due as far as standards in Amish communities went, and yet they were also well-respected. It would be a score for any young lady to marry Amos King. She would not let Naomi get in the way. Absolutely not!

She would have to be a bit coy about it, not to make people think badly of her, of course. She had her own reputation to think about too. She knew what everyone said about her, that she talked too much for her own good, but otherwise, was a nice young lady. Linda watched Amos and Naomi's small interactions through the day. She watched as Naomi specifically approached Amos near the construction zone and offered him a tall glass of water. She even caught a wide toothy smile spread across his face. That couldn't be, could it? That's when she knew what she had to do. The only thing to do was to keep Amos away from Naomi and to make Amos think that she was involved with another boy already. That Roy Miller. Why not? Roy Miller was just one year older than Naomi, and he had a crush on her for years, but she either never noticed or simply wasn't interested. If she started telling the others that Naomi and Roy were going out, Roy could jump on the opportunity to actually ask her out. That would ruin any chance of Amos and Amos becoming an "item."

As the barn was going up and the day was closing, Linda found herself a quiet corner with some of the older women in the community who lived for gossip. Some of these women barely had anything to do all day, so they discussed the potential matches for their grandchildren, their neighbor's children, and basically anyone of the age to marry. Linda found her opportunity and went for it. "You know," started Linda "Naomi and Roy are getting awfully close to each other. Have you seen the way Roy looks at Naomi? Now I know that Naomi's mother really needs the female help at home, but it's time that she is allowed to have her own life, no, what do you think?" The other ladies nodded, agreeing, and started whispering. One of the women was Naomi's great aunt, Fannie, who didn't love anything more than gossip, except perhaps warm bread. Better yet, warm bread and gossip together! Fannie whispered other women that of course, she knew that Naomi was dating Roy. She decided it was much better to appear that she knew things rather than to seem ignorant, even though she knew nothing about Naomi going out with that Roy boy. The other ladies began to gossip earnestly with a lack of concern about the damage that this new gossip could cause.

By the time the last piece of the barn roof was in place, everyone seemed to believe that Naomi and Roy were dating. It was amazing how fast fresh news traveled in a small Amish community, especially on the day of a barn-raising. Linda was a genius. She at least thought of herself that way, as she was more than satisfied that her plan to keep Amos and Naomi apart was already working. It appeared that the news had reached even Amos' ears. Linda watched from afar as Naomi looked to say good night to Amos. Amos had seen Naomi but after hearing the news that she was already courting another, he decided to respect her decision and decided that it was better if he did not speak to her further individually. After all, if Naomi was the respectful young lady that he thought she was, he did not want to be the one to ruin her dignity.

How was it possible though that he didn't know she was seeing someone else? Of course, a young, beautiful, intelligent, hard-working girl like Naomi would see something in Roy. Roy was, well Roy. He was charming, he had a sense of pride in his work, but there was something about Roy that Amos never really liked. He always wanted to impress the others and show off his work. A good Amish man was humble and rarely accepted praise let alone gave himself praise. Regardless, Amos thought it was better to respect Naomi's privacy, and snuck out with his family after dark without saying goodbye to Naomi. Naomi continued to scour the crowd until her mother insisted that they leave. Her mother also having heard the gossip knew that it was time to go home. What a day, she would have to speak to her daughter in private. The family just couldn't handle gossip like this. If there was any shred of truth to her daughter seeing Roy, well she should have been the first to know!

**Chapter 7: Real Talk**

Rebekah decided not to speak to her daughter until the next day. For certain her daughter had her the gossip too and she was worried because her little romance was discovered. And all along she had thought that her daughter was interested in the Amos King boy. Actually, Roy was not at all a suitable husband for her daughter and she simply wouldn't have it. She secretly liked the idea of her daughter marrying a King, even if it was the name only. Amos King was a nice young man and she had no reason to not let her daughter date him, except of course the fact that eventually she would be swept off her feet, and she would be all alone with a house full of boys. Even her husband was child-like sometimes and life would just not be the same without her daughter. She was hard on her daughter because she loved her, but she realized that even Naomi would want a family of her own someday. She just had hoped that it wouldn't happen quite this soon.

When dawn broke the next morning, Rebekah knocked on her daughter's bedroom door. Since she was the only girl she was lucky enough to get her own room. Privacy and all those things. Before puberty, it wasn't a problem for her to share a room with some of the boys, but now, those days were quite long gone. "Naomi, I know you're in there, come on now, this is enough, we have to talk. Naomi!" shouted Rebekah. Finally, Rebekah simply tried to door. It came open immediately and was unlocked. Naomi had already risen and was perhaps already tending to her chores. "Better," thought Rebekah, "maybe I can knock some sense into this girl!"

Rebekah marched herself toward their small barn where they kept their cow, Bella, and found Naomi in a pile on the ground, crumpled up, crying like a rag doll. "Get up! Naomi! Now!" screeched her mother. Naomi stood up and continued sobbing. "Whatever this nonsense is with Roy it stops," said Rebekah. "Understood?" she asked her daughter. "What, what?" said Naomi, finding a way to choke out a few words between the tears rolling down her face. "Roy? I don't even like Roy! He's such a rude boy! Who do you listen to these days? Me! Or everyone else?" shouted Naomi. Rebekah's mother feeling slightly bad that she had upset her daughter said, "Come inside, let's have a cup of tea. Let's go, now." Rebekah pulled her daughter off the ground and all but drug her inside the house. She then set a pot of water on the wood-burning stove and allowed Naomi to compose herself for a moment. "Let's start from the beginning," said Rebekah. "What's going on?" she asked. Naomi replied "Nothing. Except that I'm supposedly dating Roy or whatever, and yeah... I'm not ok, thanks for asking."

"Do you like that Amos boy?" asked Rebekah. "Um, yeah I think so," replied Naomi, as she slumped both further into her chair and in despair. "Well, you know, I need your help around here, Naomi, but what can I say, I can't keep you here forever. You are old enough to start dating, although, I'd be happy to keep you here as long as you'd like to stay here with me single forever!" joked Naomi's mother. "Um, Mom. That's sort of exactly what I'm afraid of, but thanks for making me feel worse, Mom," replied Naomi. "Ok, my dear, look, I do want you to be happy, you know that, right?" said Rebekah. "Yeah, I guess," answered Naomi. "Well then, don't you have some dolls to deliver?" asked Rebekah. "But, how... how do you know that I was making those dolls for Amos' cousins?" stammered Naomi. "I wasn't born yesterday my dear, I knew they had something to do with that King boy," she said. "Right, I'll be back soon," Naomi replied.

Naomi's mother watched Naomi get ready in a hurried fashion, threw her backpack over her shoulder, and flew out the door with her mother shouting something behind her that got carried away by the wind. Naomi's mother had shouted "Don't be too late for dinner!" but her words were lost on Naomi. Rebekah knew that her daughter wasn't listening, but if she wanted to date Amos King, what could she say... he was a good boy after all, and they certainly had more cows than they did, which wasn't hard to do since they had only one! Rebekah's mother chuckled to herself thinking about how her daughter was all grown up, well, almost.

**Chapter 8: Doll Delivery**

Naomi was almost shaking as she walked up to the door on the King's house. She hadn't announced that she was coming. It was less than 24 hours since the barn-raising, but now, for certain, everyone believed that she was dating that awful Miller boy. She had to set things straight, that she wanted to date Amos. Amos didn't answer the door when she rang the doorbell. Naomi looked up to find one of Amos' younger sisters at the door. "Moooooooom, that girl is here again," she shouted. Amos' mother, Faith King, a quiet, composed woman came to the door and asked Naomi to step inside. "Why, Naomi, you certainly have been the talk of the town, please why are you visiting us today?" asked Faith King. "Sorry, Ma'am, I just wanted to deliver something to Amos that I promised him I would make for his cousins. Can you please just give him this bag?" asked Naomi. "Better yet, why don't you step inside. Can I get you something to eat or drink?" she asked. "No Ma'am, please just tell Amos I was here," Naomi answered.

Just as Naomi turned to leave, Amos peered from behind the door. Amos didn't say anything, he just looked at her with disappointment and walked back inside the house. As Naomi turned toward the sidewalk she felt tears fall from her eyes. After Naomi had turned around and started walking away, Amos could see the sadness in her step and started to believe that he had been deceived, yet he did not call her to come back.

Inside the King's house, Faith King sat with her son Amos, like any good mother would do, and simply said, "I don't believe so much that a nice girl like Naomi would date a boy like Roy, now do you?" Having said all she needed to say, she handed her son the bag full of dolls that Naomi had made by hand for Amos' younger cousins. Amos took the bag, smiled sheepishly and plopped himself down in his favorite reading and thinking chair. He sighed a little, seeing as he did not have any younger cousins. Actually, his sister-in-law was expecting a baby in a few months, but the baby wouldn't be playing with dolls for a while. He couldn't believe how quickly he fell for her smile, her charm, her beauty. How could all of this be unfolding so terribly he thought to himself.

**Chapter 9: Do or Don't**

Naomi returned to her house in time for dinner, but her mother immediately knew the outcome had not been as desired. Neither Naomi nor her mother spoke about their previous discussion as dinner continued. There was a silence at the table, aside from a few requests to pass the water, the salt, and the meat. Naomi sulked all week in her home. Even when she was feeding the chickens she found herself working in complete silence when she would usually sing. You could say Amos fared worse, as he started to feel bad that he had not even received her inside the house when she arrived with the dolls that he requested her to make, nor had he offered her any jars of homemade peanut butter in exchange. One good for another. Amos worked on the farm, as usual, manual labor kept him from going a little crazy.

He found that no matter what he did his mind returned to Naomi. He was determined at the next church singing to ask to drive her home in the family's horse and buggy. The next church singing would be in three days. He knew he needed to talk to her then or he would never forgive himself. After the church service at the Stoltzfus's house, there was another church singing for the youth to gather and mingle like usual. Not even 15 minutes after the service was over, Linda found her way through the crowd to Amos.

"So, Amos, what do you know, Naomi and Roy, huh?" "Yeah, um, sure, I don't know," said Amos. "But I think they're cute together, don't you?" stated Linda, attempting to affirm her lie that Naomi and Roy were a couple. "Actually, I don't even know if they're together. I've never seen them together," he said. "Oh. Well, anyway, everyone knows they're together now," said Linda. "Ok, well, have a nice evening Linda," said Amos politely as he turned and walked away. Linda, outraged, found herself abandoned in the middle of her conversation with Amos. Her plan to ruin Naomi and Amos didn't seem to be taking hold like she thought! Wretched girl! What went wrong?

As Linda turned she saw Amos speaking with Naomi almost immediately. "Naomi, I... I don't know what came over me the other day and I'm..." Amos was cut off speaking as Linda made her way across the room towards them angrily. "Don't you know that you two are supposed to be angry at each other!!!" she yelled. All of a sudden, Linda realized that she, in fact, had just made a fool of herself. Instead of everyone looking at Amos and Naomi, or even Roy, they were all staring at Linda. Linda quickly composed herself and said, "Well, have a nice evening!"

As soon as Linda was gone from immediate sight and earshot, Amos asked Naomi, "Can I take you home tonight after the singing, if you're free?" Naomi said, "Oh, I have to ask my Mom first." "Actually, I already asked her for you, and she said yes," replied Amos. "Really?" asked Naomi. "Yes," said Amos as his cheeks grew completely red with color. "Well then, that's definitely a yes. Maybe we can sit outside on the balcony and have something to eat? Do you like to look at the stars? I love star gazing." "Sure, actually I just want to spend some time with you, if that's okay." "That would be lovely," she replied.

Amos excused himself from Naomi and mingled with some of his friends, as Naomi did the same. She found herself gleefully telling Ruth in the corner, everything that happened and how Amos was taking her home this evening. As the evening closed, Naomi waited slightly impatiently outside the gathering. The palms of her hands were sweaty just thinking about touching his hands. Amos approached her quietly, and placed the thick of his hand on the small of her back, a little too low to be only a friendly interest. Amos walked Naomi to the carriage and opened the door for to step inside. "What about your brothers and sisters?" asked Naomi, "How are they going home?" "Oh, don't worry about them, they can walk home from here," replied Amos. "So, it's just you and me then?" questioned Naomi. "It would seem so." Amos prepared the horses and they rode off into the night towards Naomi's home.

# AMBER & ABEL

109

## MONICA MARKS

## Amber and Abel
### Milan, Italy

"No! No! No!" Amber cried, throwing her hands up in dismay. "How did this happen? How *could* this happen?"

The others in the hung their heads in unison, no one willing to accept the blame for the most recent catastrophe.

"Giuliana is to wear the taffeta number, Gia the silk and Corina the leather and lace. Who screwed this up? Come on, speak up. Time is money, people!"

Again, only mollified silence met the designer's question.

Amber stifled a groan, knowing that she would not get an admission from the group.

"Never mind now," she sighed. "Twenty minutes to curtain. Get the models re-dressed at once. Keep an eye on the rotation! It's simple reading! It's not that complicated!"

A chorus of "yes ma'am" filled her ears and she spun to deal with the next mishap as someone shoved a clipboard in her face.

*It doesn't matter how many years I've been doing this, I have yet to see a fashion show go as planned.*

It was not for lack of excruciating planning of course. Every detail had been mapped to the last second months in advance and yet inevitably, someone impetrative would call in sick or a top investor would want to bring his six grandchildren backstage. Invariably, a model vomited on the runway or a make-up artist and hair stylist got into a fist fight.

It was what kept Amber's blood pressure skyrocketing and her heart rushing in her ears.

"Amber! Amber, you have an urgent phone call!"

Her assistant, Dana appeared, holding out one of the three cell phones she carried but Amber waved her away.

Every phone call was an urgent phone call. It was an occupational hazard.

"Not now, Dana. Can't you see we're T minus nineteen minutes?"

"Amber, you need to take – "

"Dana! I am up to my ears in disasters right now. Can you please deal with whatever it is? Is that not what I pay you the big bucks for?"

For a timeless second, a hush seemed to fall over the bustling backstage and inexplicably, Amber felt the hairs on her arms raise as she lifted her head.

She looked at Dana who shook her head quietly.

"What is it?" Amber breathed. "What happened?"

Dana visibly swallowed, lowering her kind, brown eyes through the lenses of her glasses.

She extended the phone further.

"It's your mother."

And Amber's world stopped.

**<u>Brooklyn, New York</u>**

"I'm looking for Leah Colville," Amber told the nurse. She drummed her fingers anxiously on the counter as the woman punched in the information and nodded.

"Room 717," she announced. "Just follow that hallway to the end."

Amber barely heard the last words as she flew down toward her mother's room.

It was slightly ajar and she pushed it open, her stomach flipping nervously.

"Mama?" she called softly. "Mama, are you awake?"

"Amber?"

She hurried inside the semi-private room, sliding the separating curtain aside.

Leah was the only one in the room but Amber knew that could change at the drop of a hat.

*Oh mama, why didn't you say anything?*

Her breath caught in her throat as she stared at her one virile mother, sunken in the bed, her face as white as the sterile sheets in which she lay.

Amber threw herself into her mother's arms gently.

"Oh mama," she whispered. "Why didn't you tell me it had gotten so bad?"

Leah made a dismissive sound with her tongue.

"You are a busy girl, Amber. The last thing you need is your old, sick mom crying in your ear about chemo treatments and hair loss. It's nothing you haven't heard a million times before."

Tears filled Amber's grey eyes but she hid them.

"I am never too busy for you," she scolded tenderly. "How long have you been like this?"

Leah sighed.

"Three weeks. The doctors are shocked I've hung on this long, kitten. It's only a matter of time..."

A stunning bolt of guilt almost brought Amber to her knees.

*How could I not have known for three weeks? What kind of daughter am I?*

"Don't talk like that!" Amber cried. "You're not going to..."

She trailed off as her voice caught in her throat.

"Shh, kitten. Don't cry now. We have both known that I have been living on borrowed time for a long while. God has been gracious enough to let me see you become successful and now I can go to the other side knowing you are secure."

Amber pursed her lips together, squeezing her mom's frail body.

"But I need you to do something for me," the older Colville woman continued and Amber raised her head.

"Anything, mama. Tell me what you need."

Leah studied her beautiful daughter's face for a long moment, reaching up to stroke her short, layered hair.

"Two things actually."

Amber stared at her expectantly.

"First, when I die, I need you to go to Pennsylvania and find my sister, Ruthie to let her know I've passed."

Amber stared at her uncomprehendingly.

"Your sister Ruthie?" she echoed. "Since when do you have a sister Ruthie?"

Leah offered her a weak smile.

"I have always had a sister, kitten."

Amber waited for her to elaborate but Leah seemed to have lost her strength suddenly.

"I'm tired, Amber," she murmured. "I would like to rest now."

"Yes, mama, of course," Amber replied, sitting up. "I will be right here when you wake up."

Leah patted her daughter's hand and smiled lovingly.

"The second thing I would like you to do it grow your hair long again. I miss those golden locks of yours."

Amber forced a smile through the tears in her eyes.

"I will do that mama. I will grow my hair and find Aunt Ruthie in Pennsylvania."

Leah nodded slowly, her eyes growing heavy.

"Just Ruthie, not Aunt Ruthie. You can find her in Eden, Pennsylvania. Ruthie Miller."

Amber watched with a trembling chin as her mother's eyes fell closed knowing that it was the last time she would ever see them open again.

### <u>Eden, Pennsylvania</u>

Amber looked at the woman embarrassed.

"I'm afraid I don't know much more than what I've already told you," Amber admitted, wishing away the clerk's scornful scrutiny. "My mother asked me to find her sister here in Eden and I have no idea where to start."

The clerk gave her a look which was half bemused, half annoyed but she turned back to her computer.

"Ruth Miller," she sighed, shaking her head. "There has to be at least two dozen here and that's only the ones we have one record."

Amber blinked and stared at her.

"This is city hall, isn't it? Why wouldn't you have them on record? Do you have a lot of illegal immigrants here?"

Amber's question was sincere but the clerk's expression turned sardonic.

"You really are not from around here, are you?"

Amber swallowed her annoyance and forced a smile.

"No, ma'am. I am not. That is why any help you can give me would be greatly appreciated. Why would you not have someone on record?"

"This is Amish country, honey."

Amber suddenly felt foolish and she grinned sheepishly.

"Of course. Well, can you see if any of the Ruth Millers you have there have a sister named Leah?"

The clerk's red eyebrows rose almost to her hairline.

"Ruth and Leah Miller? Are you kidding me? You're definitely looking for an Amish family, sweetie."

"That can't be," Amber said shaking her head. "My mom wasn't Amish."

"Well, I can check but if it quacks like a duck..."

Again, her fingers flew over the keyboard and she raised an eyebrow.

"I have two Ruth Millers with a sibling named Leah."

She scrawled their telephone numbers onto a piece of paper for her.

"But I wouldn't get your hopes up, honey," the clerk told her as she held out the sheet. "My guess is that your Ruth Miller is somewhere in the countryside."

Amber stared at her helplessly.

"What do I do then?"

"If neither of these women is who you're seeking, I would start combing the districts."

Amber opened her mouth to ask what that meant but the older woman seemed irritated enough.

She closed her mouth and vowed to find someone else to help her find answers.

Instead, she thanked her and hurried out of the building, into the windy autumn day.

As she stood on the steps, looking down at the phone numbers in her hands, a memory flittered through her mind.

She had been about four years old and her mother pulled a long dress from a hope chest at the foot of the bed.

It had been just after Amber's father had died and Leah had been so melancholic, digging through old photos and keepsakes.

"That's an old dress, mama," Amber said, looking at the homespun fabric in awe.

"It is, kitten, yes," her mother agreed. "Would you like to try it on?"

"Yes please!" Amber cried and Leah had laughed, slipping the too large garment onto her small daughter.

The older Colville dug into the chest and removed a small white cap, placing it on the base of Amber's head.

"You look like a proper Amish girl now, *Liebchen*."

"What is an Amish girl, mama?"

"Greta!"

The voice was loud and almost directly in her ear, smashing her reverie into a million pieces.

Startled, Amber turned to look.

An Amish man stood behind her, his green eyes alight with hope as she met his stare.

"Greta, you've returned!" he said excitedly. "When did you come back to Eden?"

Amber shook her head.

"I'm sorry," she said kindly, still awed by the green of his irises. "You have me confused with someone else."

To her surprise, his brow furrowed and he scowled slightly.

"Are you playing a game?" he asked gruffly, his eyes narrowing. "You don't need to worry; I won't tell anyone I have seen you."

Amber's eyes widened and she wondered if she was in the middle of a gag.

She looked around for cameras but nothing seemed out of the ordinary.

"I really am sorry," she said again, continuing down the steps. "You have me mixed up with someone else. My name isn't Greta."

She hurried away before he could respond, leaving him staring after her.

As she made her way toward the street where her rental car waited, she glanced back uneasily at the attractive man, her heart racing.

*That was strange,* she thought, sliding into the driver's side.

But as she pulled away from the curb, she wondered if it was less strange and more fate.

Perhaps that man was God's way of telling her that she would find her long lost aunt inside the Amish community after all.

*I guess it's time to start combing the districts,* Amber thought wryly. *Whatever that means.*

She could not help but take one last peek at the man in her rear-view as she drove away. He remained standing on the steps, staring after her as if he expected her to return.

*I hope he finds Greta,* she thought wistfully. *He certainly seems to love her.*

"Abel, who was that?" Levi demanded, rushing up the steps of city hall to meet his brother. He peered in the direction which the car gone.

"Apparently no one," Abel muttered as he watched the small sports car zoom away from the center of town.

"From where I stood, it looked to be Greta Shetler and – "

"It was not," Abel snapped, cutting off his brother before another word could leave his lips.

Levi eyed him warily.

"You seem upset," he commented. "Hasn't that woman done enough damage to you without having you pine for her?"

"Let's not speak about her," Abel said between clenched teeth as he hurried down the steps. "We have errands to run."

Levi chuckled dryly.

"Well whoever she is, I would not mind seeing her again," Levi commented. Abel paused to give his brother a scathing look.

"She is an Englisher," he retorted. "You would do well to stay away from her."

"Why? Are you interested?" Levi mocked. "And I thought you were going to die longing for the shunned and shamed beauty of the district."

"You are speaking nonsense now, Levi," Abel chided. "If you can't speak normally, don't speak at all."

Abel didn't have to look over to know his brother was leering at him.

It seemed everyone in town had been ogling him since the day Greta had run off with the Englisher, leaving him at the altar after declaring she was pregnant with the Englisher's child.

And now she was back, pretending that she did not recognize him.

It was just another slap in the face after her ex-communication, almost two years earlier.

*Has she come back to humiliate me further?*

"Who was she if not Greta?" Levi demanded, obviously unwilling to leave the topic alone.

"You know you should not even be speaking her name," Abel snapped. "I don't know who that woman was."

"Then why did you run after her if you don't know her?"

Abel was growing angry with his brother's interrogation.

"Let us go our own way today. We can accomplish more that way."

Without permitting Levi an opportunity to answer, he rushed away, trying to leave his brother in his wake along with the painful memories of Greta.

After finding a quiet spot to park her car, Amber picked up her cell phone.

She tried both the phone numbers given to her by the clerk at city hall but as the woman had predicted, neither was the woman Amber sought.

*Now I have to venture from district to district,* she realized. She was not looking forward to the task; it seemed daunting but she knew she could not rest until she had honored her mother's wishes.

Instinctively, she reached up and touched her hair.

It had already begun to grow out some in the two months since Leah's passing and Amber was determined not to touch it.

As she drove the rental into the outskirts of Eden, the lush Pennsylvania hills fell into a smaller settlement of land and soon, she could see that she was inside the Amish district.

Almost immediately, a feeling of peace overcame her and she had to stop the car to admire the almost surreal beauty of the landscape around her.

She grabbed for her cell phone, snapping pictures as the horizon as the sun began to set over the lolling dales.

Suddenly, she heard the clopping of hooves as a wagon approached and Amber lowered her camera, watching in awe as a horse and cart ambled toward her.

In the front, a man and woman dressed in traditional Amish attire rode primly and Amber offered them a nervous smile, not knowing if she would be received with distain.

To her relief, they both returned her beam and the man slowed the beast.

"Are you lost, miss?" he asked politely and Amber shook her head.

"No...well maybe," she replied sheepishly. "I stopped to take a picture of the beautiful landscape but..."

She trailed off, suddenly embarrassed.

"I am afraid I'm on a bit of a wild goose chase," she confessed. They peered at her with curious eyes.

"Are you looking for someone's home?" the woman asked. "Perhaps we can direct you."

Amber opened her mouth to answer and then closed it.

"This is going to seem ridiculous," she muttered. "But I am looking for a woman named Ruthie Miller. Do you know her?"

The couple seemed slightly amused by the question and Amber was beginning to realize that was going to be a common response to her inquiry.

*I wonder what it would be like to live in a place where everyone knew everyone else? I imagine there is a sense of security that accompanies that knowledge.*

"I fear that we know several women by that name, miss. Can you tell us anything else about her?"

"She had a sister named Leah but they have been estranged for – "

Suddenly, Amber found it difficult to speak and she swallowed quickly as her voice broke.

"Have you had supper, miss?" the woman asked quietly. "Our farm is not far from here. It would be our pleasure to have you as our guest."

Amber looked up, terrified and shook her head.

"Oh no, I couldn't," she gulped. "But thank you."

The man smiled.

"It is considered very rude to refuse a supper invitation in Amish country," he informed her and Amber could see he was teasing her but all the same, she found herself nodding.

"That would be lovely," she breathed. "Thank you."

"You may follow us," the woman said, smiling.

Amber nodded and allowed them to pass before jumping back into her car.

*What lovely people,* she thought, her heart warming. The man on the steps of city hall had made her nervous and so far, he had been the only interaction she had with anyone in their culture.

*But he did have lovely green eyes.*

Amber steered the Chrysler into up the long drive of the pretty farmhouse, keeping a safe distance behind the kind strangers.

Slowly, she exited her car, suddenly aware of how strange was what she was doing.

*Would I ever accept such an unexpected dinner invitation from random strangers in New York or Milan or Paris? Of course not. So why am I doing it here?*

The answer was obvious; it felt right.

She was nowhere near any major city, designing clothes and fighting with stage hands or arguing with models.

It was like she had entered another world, another planet even where Amber Colville didn't exist and she was just a lost little girl, looking for the last family relation she had left in the world.

*Does my Aunt Ruthie have children? Maybe I have cousins out there. Or should I say, in here.*

"Come along, miss. It's growing cold without the sun shining down on us," the woman urged.

"My name is Amber," she volunteered as she was led into the house. "Amber Colville."

The wife smiled and nodded.

"That is a lovely name. I am Beth and that is my husband, Jeremiah Troyer."

"Pleased to meet you, Mr. and Mrs. Troyer," I said politely.

She smiled softly.

"We do not use such formalities here. You may call us Beth and Jeremiah," she said softly.

Amber blushed lightly and nodded.

"Only if you call me Amber," she agreed.

"Please, come and sit. Our boys should be along shortly. They have been commissioned with supper as Jeremiah and I were in town today."

"I see," she said, nodding. "But you are farmers?"

"Yes," Beth replied. "We grow wheat and barley. Our boys have recently acquired chickens but between you and I, Amber, I am rather fearful of their pecking beaks."

Amber chuckled with Jeremiah.

"There is no shame in having fears, Beth," her husband said, reassuringly. "I am certain even the English have fears."

Amber's smile broadened.

"Oh yes," she assured them. "More fears than I care to admit."

A sudden warmth flowed between them as they stood in a comfortable silence.

"Come along inside," Jeremiah said, shooing them from the foyer. "I will see about some cider. It is cooling in the shed. Abel just made a fresh batch."

"He's a good boy, our eldest," Beth murmured but Amber noticed a dark cloud cross over her eyes as if something occurred to her.

She stared at Amber, her mouth parting slightly.

"Is something wrong, Beth?" Amber asked, immediately concerned by her change of disposition.

The older woman shook her head.

"I will help Jeremiah with the cider. The barrel can be difficult to manage. Please, sit by the fire until we return."

She was gone before Amber could reply and she was abruptly filled with a small fission of alarm.

*That was strange,* she thought but she was ashamed of her suspicion. *Things are just done differently here than they are in the city. There's nothing strange about it.*

"*Mamm! Daed?*"

She turned her head as a man called out, poking his head into the sitting room where Amber had sunk into a wing chair.

He seemed to freeze as he looked at her.

"Hello," Amber volunteered. "I'm Amber Colville. Your parents have invited me for dinner."

A small smile appeared on the young man's lips and he stalked toward her, extending his hand.

"Levi Troyer," he announced. "You were in Eden today, were you not?"

Surprised, Amber nodded.

"Yes, I was at city hall, looking for information."

Levi's eyebrow raised.

"What sort of information?" he asked curiously, placing himself into the chair facing her.

Amber swallowed and shook her head.

"It's not really important," she said quickly. "I would rather not get into it right now."

Levi's blue eyes narrowed slightly.

"I can be a wonderful source of information," he told her. "If you ever feel like talking."

His meaning was unmistakable and Amber found herself amused and slightly intrigued by the forward speaking man.

"Thank you," she replied, laughing. "Perhaps after dinner. It's not a very cheerful supper conversation."

"Levi, why did you leave me alone to finish supper. I have – "

Amber turned toward the doorway again and her jaw dropped.

"Wh -what is she doing here?" the man gasped, looking accusingly at his brother. Levi jumped to his feet, grinning.

"It appears as thought *Mamm* and *Daed* have invited her over for supper. Amber, this is my brother, Abel."

Cautiously, Amber rose to her feet, unsure of how Abel would react to her as she recalled their previous encounter.

"Hello Abel," she said quietly. "Pleased to meet you."

She wasn't sure if she should extend her hand or not but she found herself once more staring into his impossibly green eyes as if hypnotized.

He did not immediately respond and Amber felt her heart sink slightly as he continued to stare at her.

"Forgive my brother," Levi interceded. Amber turned questioningly to him.

"He seems to think you look like someone he knew once a long time ago," Levi offered and Amber nodded slightly.

"I never said that," Abel grumbled but Amber felt that his gaze betrayed his words. He could not seem to pull his irises from her face as if trying to memorize every feature.

"There you are," Beth said, hurrying into the front room, a concerned expression on her face. She held out a glass for Amber.

"This is apple cider from the Bachman's orchid," she told Amber, smiling briefly. The older woman seemed to sense the tension in the room.

"I see you have met our sons, Abel and Levi," she continued as Amber accepted the cup. "What have you made for supper, boys? I am sure our guest is as hungry as your father."

"What did the doctor say, *Mamm*?" Abel asked suddenly, diverting his attention to his mother.

Beth's face turned pale and angry.

"Abel, that is hardly an appropriate question to ask before visitors. Go tend to supper," she snapped with a harshness Amber was sure was not customary.

Abel seemed contrite but he disappeared, bowing his head somewhat shamefully.

Amber felt a spark of apprehension in her stomach as she cast Beth a sidelong look.

*Why did she go to the doctor? Is she ill? Does she have cancer like mama?*

Amber bit on her lower lip and tried to push the image of her mother from her mind but it was more difficult than she wished.

"Are you all right, Amber?" Beth asked, her brow furrowing deeper as she watched the blonde's face crumble.

Amber tried to nod but a tear escaped her and slid down her cheek.

"I'm sorry," the younger woman told the others, quickly wiping the streak from her face. "I recently lost my mother and I was just thinking of her. Forgive me for my display."

Beth and Levi made a commiserating noise.

"Levi, go help your brother and leave the women to talk," Beth ordered. Levi rose without protest, leaving them alone in the front room.

"It is difficult to lose a parent," Beth said comfortingly. "I have lost both of mine."

Amber sighed.

"I am so sorry, Beth. My father also died when I was very young."

Beth leaned down to pat her hand soothingly and Amber found the gesture heartwarming.

*I am a perfect stranger to her and yet she feels the need to comfort me. This place is like a television program. This isn't real life. This is a place where daughters would know that their mothers have been dying for weeks, not off running fashion shows in Italy.*

"Supper is ready, *Mamm*, Amber," Levi called from the dining room and the women rose to join the others at the dinner table.

"We pray before eating, Amber. You are not required to join us," Jeremiah told her as she took a seat across from the Troyer brothers.

"I would be happy to join in your prayer if you'll have me," Amber replied. She pretended not to notice the look of appreciation shared by the family as she hung her head.

Jeremiah lead the prayer in Pennsylvania Dutch but Amber could catch some of the key words from the time she had spent in Munich.

"You still have not told us what you are doing in our district, Gre – ah, Amber," Levi piped up after they had loaded their plates with meat, vegetables, potatoes and bread.

Beth and Jeremiah looked up sharply while Abel's jaw tightened.

"Were you going to call me Greta also?" Amber asked, her eyes widening. Levi seemed embarrassed.

"You do bear an uncanny resemblance to her," he confessed.

"I did not notice," Beth interjected, eyeing her older son.

"Nor did I!" Jeremiah agreed and there was a finality in his tone. It was clear that the subject was to be dropped and Amber did not want to push the issue.

Nevertheless, she was fascinated by the fact she might have an Amish twin.

"I have come here looking for my mother's sister but I'm afraid I don't have much to go off. I don't even know if I'm looking in the right spot but my mom only told me about her before she died."

Beth looked up and smiled.

"We told Amber we would happily help her find her aunt but we would need to narrow the search somehow."

"What is her name?"

Amber was surprised it was Abel who asked the question.

"Ruthie Miller. Her sister, my mother, was Leah."

The table fell silent as the family appeared to rake their memories.

"Well, I can think of four women by that name. One is far too young to be your aunt, one is much too old and the other two have lived in the district all their lives without a sister named Leah," Jeremiah volunteered, chewing his fried steak pensively. "Have I forgotten someone?"

"No...I do not believe you have," Beth replied. She gazed at her boys.

"Any suggestions?"

Levi shrugged his shoulders.

"As Amber has said, there is no guarantee that this Ruthie Miller is from this district. Perhaps I could take her to the neighboring districts tomorrow and we could investigate further."

He beamed at her and Amber smiled back but she could not help her gaze from falling on the older Troyer brother.

He seemed to glower into his plate, unspeaking.

"That would be lovely," Amber said reluctantly, realizing that Abel was not about to volunteer his help.

*Is he always so brooding or is it because I remind him of this Greta?*

"It's settled then. Tomorrow I will take you in search of your aunt!" Levi said jovially.

Amber could not help but notice that he gently jabbed his brother in the ribs and she wondered if she hadn't put herself in the middle of a sibling rivalry.

Abel could not sleep and he lay on his back, arms folded across his chest.

"I can feel you breathing fire over there, Abe," Levi called mockingly through the dark. "Why are you so upset?"

"I'm not!" Abel denied but Levi only laughed.

"Why don't you just admit that you want to take Amber on her search tomorrow?"

"I do not," he replied hotly but as he said the words, he knew they were a lie.

He couldn't seem to get over the remarkable likeness Amber shared to Greta. It was as if *Gotte* had sent him a chance to get things right with Greta.

*That's ridiculous. They are two different women. If Levi wishes to waste his time with an Englisher, let him do it.*

"You truly are a fool," Levi sighed, sitting up. Abel turned his head to scowl at his brother in the moonlit room.

"You would know a fool to see one, brother," he snapped. "Stop talking and let me go to sleep."

Levi groaned.

"I only offered to take Amber tomorrow because I knew you wouldn't. You will pick her up at her hotel in Eden and take her."

"I will not!" Abel was insulted at the idea of stealing his brother's date. "She has agreed to go with you, not me."

"But she wants to go with you," Levi insisted. "She could not stop staring at you all through dinner. Didn't you notice?"

Abel had not.

"Of course you didn't notice. You were too busy sulking about Greta to notice the lovely woman yearning for you to look at her. I think Amber is *Gotte's* way of telling you that it is time to move on."

"What do you know?" Abel growled but in his heart, he felt a sliver of hope.

*Is he just telling me that because he believes I have spent too much time pining over Greta or did Amber find me interesting?*

"I know that if you don't act on this opportunity, I will give you no more second chances. I will pursue Amber myself."

Abel didn't answer but his heart sank at his brother's words.

*Maybe this is a sign from Gotte. What harm can it do to take her tomorrow?*

Amber felt a spark of happiness when she saw Abel at the reins the following morning in front of the Eden Resort and Suites.

"I hope you do not mind that I have come in my brother's place," Abel said, somewhat gruffly but Amber was already learning that it was shyness, not rudeness.

"I am very happy it was you," she replied earnestly, catching his eye.

A shiver coursed down her spine as he helped her onto the wagon and they made their way out of town toward the districts.

She found herself studying his handsome profile, taking in the fine shape of his nose and delicate bone structure.

"I hope that you will not be disappointed," Abel told her as they started their ride in silence.

Amber glanced at him in surprise, thinking that he had caught her staring at him.

She blushed and shook her head.

"I'm not disappointed in the least," she replied, lowering her eyes.

He shot her a sidelong look and gave her a lopsided smile.

"I meant that I hope you find your aunt," he explained. Amber turned bright red and cleared her throat in nervousness.

"Of course," she muttered, doubly ashamed.

She had almost forgotten the reason for their drive as if they were merely on a date.

*Focus on the task at hand,* she told herself.

Soon, they were in one of the neighboring districts and Abel proved to be a wonderful guide, finding a minister to question almost immediately.

They did not find anyone to match their description in the first two districts they visited but as they made their way into the third, it was growing late in the afternoon and Amber was growing disheartened.

"I'm beginning to think this is a lost cause," Amber confessed as they searched for the home of the deacon as directed by a young girl playing hopscotch.

Despite her mounting disappointment, she could not shake the idyllic beauty of their community.

*I would give it all up to live here,* she thought as they found Deacon Roth tending to his herb garden.

"Hello, Deacon," Abel called. "I am Abel Troyer and this is my friend, Amber. We have some questions for you if you have a moment."

The deacon looked up and nodded, smiling welcomingly.

"Of course," he agreed. "What can I help you with?"

"Deacon, have you a Ruthie Miller who lives here? She would be in her forties or fifties with an estranged sister named Leah?"

The elderly man's mouth parted and he stared at Amber for a long moment.

"Indeed," he murmured. "Are you Ruthie's daughter?"

Amber shook her head.

"No...I am Leah's daughter," Amber replied, glancing nervously at Abel. "Do you know them?"

The man nodded thoughtfully.

"Of course, I remember Leah. She never was baptized. She fell in love with an Englisher and married him when she was nineteen or so."

Amber nodded excitedly.

"Yes! Alexander Colville. That was my father," Amber gushed. "Is Ruthie still here?"

"No, child. Ruthie was married to a man named Samuel Miller but he died in a terrible accident not two years after the wedding. That was about a year after Leah had left the district."

Amber found her palms sweating and she wiped them on her jeans.

"Where did she go? Did my aunt leave the community too?"

The deacon chuckled.

"No, no. She eventually remarried and moved on to another district."

"Nearby?" Amber pressed, her excitement mounting.

*I'm so close to finding your sister, mama!* She thought, her heart racing.

"Yes, two districts across."

Abel's face turned confused.

"Closest to Eden?" he asked and the older man nodded.

"But that's our district," Abel murmured. A look of understanding crossed his face.

"Who did she marry when she moved?" he asked.

The deacon thought for a long moment, digging into the depth of his swiss cheese memory bank.

"Ah yes. David Shetler. As far as I know, they still live there but I confess, I am out of touch sometimes," Deacon Roth chortled.

Abel's face turned grey.

"Do you know these people, Abel?" Amber asked excitedly. "Do you know where I can find them?"

He looked at her, his face aghast.

"Yes," he whispered. "I know them. They are Greta's parents. You are Greta's cousin."

The ride back to Eden was long and quiet as Abel tried to gather his thoughts. To his relief, Amber did not push him to speak as if she could sense he needed the quiet.

*Is this a cruel joke? Sending me a cousin of the woman who broke my heart? One who looks so much like her?*

But as they continued the journey back, Abel suddenly realized that he had been blinded by Amber's outward appearance.

True, she looked like Greta with the solemn grey eyes as sunny blonde hair but how similar were the two really?

Greta could not seem to run away fast enough, sacrificing her own values to do so while Amber embraced her mother's home and heritage in tribute.

Greta was selfish and hurtful while Amber was kind and loving.

Greta was gone and Amber was right there beside him, waiting for him to speak, to make the next step.

"It is getting late," he finally told her. "I don't think it is wise to interrupt your aunt at this hour although I am certain she will be happy to see you, regardless of the time."

Amber nodded but he could see the sadness in her eyes.

"That's fine. I can find my own way there tomorrow," she replied, trying to sound cheerful. "But I appreciate all your help."

She turned her head quickly but he knew it was only so he wouldn't see the tears in her eyes.

He paused, searching for the next words to say.

Opening his mouth, his perfectly concocted statement flew into the air.

"I am hungry," he said instead.

Amber turned to glance at him.

"You're hungry?" she repeated. "Oh."

She wasn't quite sure what to make of the statement.

"Me too," she replied suddenly.

Their eyes met and they smiled.

"May I buy you dinner, Amber?" he asked her sweetly.

"Like a date?" she teased.

His smiled faded and he nodded solemnly.

"Exactly like a date," he replied.

# AN AMISH HOMECOMING

## STEPHANIE SWIFT

David Montgomery walked the aisles of Alexander Mercantile & Grocery, shuffling about aimlessly while country music streamed from the overhead speakers. He'd picked up several items and given them the once-over before putting them back on the shelves with a dissatisfied grunt. If he were visiting a hardware store or lumber yard, this shopping trip would be a breeze, but trying to decide which brand of flour to buy for his mother's chicken pot pie recipe? He didn't have a clue.

He closed his eyes and groaned again. There was only one logical way to choose, but before he could eenie-meenie-miney-moe his way through it, he heard the soft sound of laughter from someone close by. David turned to find a young woman dressed in Amish clothing standing a few feet away, sorting through a shelf lined with oils and spices.

Peeking from beneath her white bonnet was a head full of long red hair, which was gathered at the nape of her neck with a blue ribbon. The bright red shade was a shocking contrast to her milky complexion and light blue eyes and gave her the appearance of a porcelain doll. The beautiful resemblance left him momentarily speechless, and when she walked over and picked up a small bag of flour and put it in his cart, he forced himself to stop gawking at her like a smitten teenager.

"If you're shopping for Miss Rosemary, you better get this brand or she'll tan your hide."

The mention of his mother's name brought him back to reality. It shouldn't have surprised him, given that there was only one Amish community in the vicinity – the same one his mother belonged to – and everyone knew each other by name.

"I apologize for the intrusion. I live a couple of houses down from Miss Rosemary," she said. "I'm Faith Somers."

She held out her hand, and David cleared his throat as he shook her hand and forced a smile. He noticed right away how soft and smooth her skin was, but her handshake was unusually firm and a lot like most of the men he'd met, which caught him off guard.

"David Montgomery. It's nice meeting you."

She nodded. "I recognized you from your photo. Miss Rosemary brags on you all the time."

David's thoughts flashed to the framed pictures of him his mother kept in her living room, and he felt his cheeks heat. They ranged from ages one to eighteen, and each year was more embarrassing than the one before.

"Well, I'll let you get back to your shopping. Have a blessed day, Mr. Montgomery!"

Before he had the chance to reply, she brushed past him and continued down the aisle without another glance in his direction. When she turned the corner and disappeared, David furrowed a brow. *Mr. Montgomery*? He hadn't heard that endearment since Bishop Luke presided over his father's funeral two years prior. Just how old did Faith Somers think he was?

David gathered the remaining items on his mother's shopping list and made his way to the checkout counter. He'd been in Dayton only three days, and he'd already talked to more people from the small Amish village than he could ever recall from the short time he lived there. So much for staying under the radar.

As an elderly gentleman scanned his groceries, David's gaze went to the large bulletin board on the wall behind the counter where several classified ads were posted. One in particular, with the headline CARPENTER NEEDED, caught his attention. The flyer's edges were tattered and worn, and the paper was faded, giving him the impression it had been on the board for quite some time.

"Excuse me, but do you happen to know the person who posted that ad?"

He pointed to the flyer in question, and when the cashier glanced at it, he shook his head. "Carson Andrews," he replied. "He was needing someone to help built a fence around his property, but that was a couple of months ago. Haven't seen him in here since then, so I don't know if he still needs the help or not."

When the man gave him his change and receipt, David scribbled the phone number from the flyer on the back of it. With any luck, the job would still be available. It wouldn't hurt to give it a shot.

"If you're looking for work, I might have something for you."

David turned toward the familiar voice and found Faith Somers standing behind him. As he folded the receipt and stuffed it inside the breast pocket of his shirt, she began unloading her shopping basket onto the counter. She stood so close he could almost count every one of her long, beautiful eyelashes.

David took a cautious step backward. "What did you have in mind?"

She smiled at him, and he could just barely make out the indention of dimples in her cheeks, which he had to admit was rather adorable.

"I inherited my grandfather's house when he passed away last year, and I've been meaning to hire someone to renovate the kitchen cabinets. Would you be interested?"

The thought of being in close quarters with a beauty like Faith intrigued him but also made him a little leery. After leaving the Amish way of life and starting over in a different city several miles away, the last thing he needed was someone or something tempting him to stay. Then again, for all he knew she might be married. If that was the case, then he was being ridiculous for no reason.

"Sounds good to me. When should I start?"

The cashier bagged her groceries and as Faith looped the handles over her right arm, he caught the elderly man watching them with an amused look on his face.

"Can you come by tomorrow morning, say around 9:00?"

He agreed, and as Faith made her way to the exit, he turned to look at the cashier, who was still smiling like a kid who'd been caught with his hand in a cookie jar.

"Do you know something I don't?" he asked.

The man looked down at the floor and chuckled before peering at David over his eyeglasses and giving him a look that teetered on the brink of sympathy. "All I'm going to say is good luck because I have a feeling you're going to need it."

With that, he turned and walked toward the back of the store. He never stopped laughing, and David couldn't help but wonder what he'd just gotten himself into.

He frowned. Perhaps he shouldn't have accepted the job so hastily, but unfortunately, there was no turning back now.

* * * *

The next morning, Faith put her hands on her hips and gave the kitchen faucet a resentful glare. She'd spent the past hour trying to replace the outdated equipment, but so far, the rusty nuts and bolts wouldn't budge. She gazed at her surroundings and let out a resigned sigh. Since the day she'd moved into her grandfather's old farmhouse, she'd been met with one obstacle after another. The ornery faucet shouldn't have come as much of a surprise, but it was more of an annoyance than anything. For once, she just wished something would go smoothly.

A loud knock on the front door startled Faith as she wiped the sweat from her brow and attempted to smooth the wrinkles on the front of her dress. She knew she probably looked a fright after her tug-of-war with the faucet, but at the moment she was too irritated to care what David Montgomery thought of her appearance.

Faith rolled her eyes heavenward. No, that wasn't the truth. After meeting him the day before, she hadn't been able to concentrate on anything else, so she actually cared a little bit too much what he might think of her.

She tucked a couple of wayward tendrils behind her ears and took a deep breath before opening the front door. David stood on the other side with a toolbox in one hand and a plate of cookies wrapped in plastic wrap in the other. It was odd seeing an English man standing on her front porch, and the sight of one in jeans and a t-shirt made her heart thump a little faster.

"Mom wouldn't let me leave the house without these, so I hope you like oatmeal cookies."

When he handed her the plate, their fingers grazed for a split second, but it was enough to make the tiny hairs on the back of her neck stand at attention. She stepped to the side to let him enter, and when he walked inside, she caught the faint scent of his cologne – a woodsy, masculine scent that tickled her senses and made her knees tremble.

"I love anything Miss Rosemary cooks," she replied. "Thank you."

As they stood facing each other in the tiny den, she was immediately struck by how tall and broad-shouldered he was. He looked larger than life, especially given their close proximity, and Faith tried in vain not to stare. When he suddenly closed the small gap between them and pressed his fingers against her right cheek, she thought for certain her heart would pound right out of her chest.

"You've got something on your cheek," he remarked. "Is that rust?"

He gently wiped the smudge away, and the heat from his touch made her light-headed as she cleared her throat and nodded.

"I've been trying to replace the kitchen faucet, and it hasn't been going very well."

She used his question as a chance to flee from the close quarters of the den and into a different room with more space to move around – and less room for touching. The kitchen was the largest room in the house, and as she motioned for him to follow her, she stayed two steps ahead of him and remained at arm's length as much as possible.

David placed his toolbox on the dining room table and looked around the room. "I see the problem," he replied with a grin. "These cabinets look like they rolled in with the Titanic."

His whole face lit up every time he smiled, and it was quite endearing and made the butterflies flip-flop inside her stomach.

"Everything in this house is ancient," she said. "I'm afraid it's going to take forever to renovate it the way I want to."

David opened his toolbox and took out a wrench, which he used to loosen the nuts and bolts on the kitchen faucet. After fighting with it for over an hour, Faith was dumbfounded when he had it completely taken apart in less than five minutes.

"There we go. Now, where is the new one?"

Faith shook her head as she placed the oatmeal cookies on a metal rack inside the refrigerator. "David, I appreciate the help, but you don't have to worry with that."

He shooed her comment away with a wave of his hand. "I don't mind. I bought an old ranch house that was in foreclosure when I moved away from here, so I know how time-consuming it can be. I'm happy to help."

Faith retrieved her shopping bag from Alexander Mercantile and pulled out the box containing the new faucet fixture. When she handed it over to David, he took to the task like a duck to water while she sat down at the dining room table and made mental notes for the other fixtures that needed replacing.

"Were you able to sell it?" she asked.

He stopped for a moment and gave her a quizzical look. "My house? Why would I do that?"

Faith was confused. From everything she'd been told, David had moved back permanently to care for his mother, but perhaps she'd misunderstood somehow.

"I'm sorry. I thought you were planning on staying here with Miss Rosemary."

David gave her a half-hearted smile, but he didn't reply right away, so she watched in silence as he tightened the bolts on the new fixture and made some other small adjustments before returning his wrench to the toolbox.

"I work in Franklin with the local fire department, and I just took a temporary leave of absence. I hope I'll be able to go back within the next two or three weeks."

For reasons she couldn't explain, his remark bothered her a lot more than she cared to admit. She wanted to say it was because she hated seeing Miss Rosemary living alone, but she knew that was only partly true. Maybe it was just her imagination, but she could have sworn there was a spark, an attraction – *something* – between the two of them, but perhaps it was one-sided. What did she know anyway? She couldn't even remember the last time a man flirted with her.

Faith stood and stuffed her hands inside her dress pockets. "I was hoping these cabinets could be painted white and the hinges and knobs replaced with something more modern. Do you think that's doable?"

He seemed taken aback by the sudden change in conversation, but she couldn't see wasting any more time on something that was unlikely to happen. If only she'd known his plans before offering him a job. With any luck, she wouldn't have to babysit him while he worked and she could stay busy doing her own thing – away from him.

David opened a couple of the cabinets and inspected the wood by running his fingertips along the grain. "It would take some sanding and a couple coats of primer, but I think they would look great painted."

Faith muddled through the next thirty minutes or so in a daze as they discussed color options and how long it would take to finish the job. She focused on other things in the room while they talked so she wouldn't be forced to concentrate on his piercing green eyes and the way his muscles flexed every time he moved.

When the details were sorted through, and David started working by removing the cabinet doors, she couldn't escape the house fast enough. Fortunately, she had chores to tend to outside that would keep her busy most of the day. As Faith closed the front door behind her and started the short trek to the barn, she whispered a silent plea for God to make the next two weeks go by as quickly as possible.

* * * *

David heard the commotion as soon as he walked outside, and he shook his head and laughed as he started for Faith's barn. The disgruntled groans and language that bordered on the obscene had become a common occurrence over the past two weeks, but no matter how hard he tried to help Faith with her chores, she always stubbornly refused.

David peeked his head inside the door, and he stifled another laugh as he watched her trying to milk one of the heifers. The animal was tied to a stall, and each time Faith leaned forward to grab onto her teats, the heifer would move just out of her reach. When Faith leaned over too far and fell sideways off the short wooden stool she was sitting on, David decided it was time to intervene before her temper got the best of her.

Before he could reach her, however, she kicked the stool several feet away and let out another frustrated groan that startled the heifer and rattled the tin roof.

"Whoa!" he exclaimed. "What was that about?"

He picked up the stool and brought it back to her, and he bit his tongue so he wouldn't laugh again when he discovered her sitting cross-legged on the ground with her arms staunchly crossed over her chest. She'd taken off her bonnet, and her lovely face was almost the same shade as her bright red hair. She looked like she could spit nails, and he approached her much like he did the bull in his mother's pasture – cautiously and with no sudden movements.

"I give up!" she yelled. "This cow hates me."

David set the stool down in front of her and sat down on it. "I seriously doubt that. I think she's just stubborn – kind of like someone else I know."

She flashed him a look of contempt, but he didn't waver, and they sat there in their own little battle of wills until Faith's shoulders slumped and she bowed her head.

"I don't know what I'm doing wrong. Nothing has gone right since I moved here last year. I'm starting to think I'm cursed or something."

Her voice was soft and sullen, and she looked so pitiful it made his heart ache. He wanted to console her somehow, but he had to fight the urge to take her in his arms.

"Faith, you're not cursed. I don't think you're giving yourself enough credit. I've seen how hard you work to keep this place running smoothly, and you're doing a great job. I'm sure your grandfather would be proud."

She looked up at him, and he caught a shimmer of tears in the corners of her eyes seconds before she wiped them away with her dress sleeve. If he'd learned anything in the past two weeks, it was that Faith Somers didn't want anyone seeing just how vulnerable she could be. He admired her tenacity, but sometimes he felt it did her more harm than good.

"I wish you would let me help you," he remarked.

It wasn't the first time he'd made such a request. He offered his help with the chores repeatedly, but she was adamant about doing everything herself. Faith was the most independent and stubborn woman he'd ever met, and it was admirable as much as it was irritating.

"David, I grew up with four brothers and no sisters, so I've spent most of my life trying to prove myself. My family has always treated me like a fragile wallflower, and sometimes I really believe that's why my grandfather willed this place to me. We were very close, and he knew how much I hated living in my brother's shadows."

It was the first time she'd opened up to him about something personal, and David was almost afraid to move or even breathe. He didn't want to ruin the moment, so he remained as quiet as a church mouse.

"When my family visits, it feels like they're watching and judging everything I do, so I have to stay on my toes all the time and make sure everything is perfect. It can be very tiring. I would love to have just one day to relax on my front porch with a cup of coffee and a good book."

David got off the stool and patted it with his hand. She sounded so downtrodden it was breaking his heart, and he was determined to help her in some way, even if she fought him kicking and screaming.

"What?" she asked.

She straightened her spine and was immediately on the defensive, as usual. Undeterred, David pat the stool again. "Come on. We're going to do this together, and you can either do it willingly, or I'll sit here and wait as long as I need to."

It didn't take as long as he expected it would, and with another one of her agitated groans, she sat down on the stool while he stood and took hold of the rope tied loosely around the heifer's neck. He coaxed the animal into position beside Faith before rubbing his hands over her head and down her neck.

"Now, I want you gently rub her stomach," he directed.

Faith crossed her arms over her chest again and gave him an incredulous look. "You can't be serious."

David tried to be as stern with her as he could. "You can attract more flies with honey than vinegar. Would you want someone with an attitude touching you?"

His question made her blush, and David immediately wished he'd worded the question differently. He didn't mean for it to come out sounding as flirty as it did, but she wasn't frowning anymore, so that was something. Faith placed her small hands against the heifer's stomach and moved them around in slow circles.

"She needs to feel like she can trust you, so take your time and don't rush," he whispered. "Rubbing her fur will help warm your hands too. They don't care for cold hands when it comes to milking."

He was trying to explain the technique as delicately as possible, so as not to offend her, but her cheeks reddened again. He felt like he should apologize, but before he had the opportunity, Faith started humming a soft tune and caught him off guard. He didn't recognize the song, but it was quite beautiful and seemed to lull the animal into submission.

David kept a firm grip on the rope while Faith placed a metal bucket under the heifer and began milking her. She continued humming throughout the entire process and the animal never flinched or tried to move away. He had to admit he was impressed. She stole a glance in his direction and when she flashed him a genuine smile, his heart thumped wildly inside his chest. When the bucket was full, she moved it out of the way and stood up slowly so as not to startle the heifer. She caressed the animal's back for several minutes, and when she stopped and took a step back, David felt like breaking into a raucous round of applause.

"That was amazing!" he exclaimed. "Well done!"

He noticed she stood a little straighter and jutted her chin out, like she was pleased with her accomplishment, and the change in her demeanor made him smile.

"Thank you, David. Your guidance made all the difference."

He could tell by the tone of her voice that it was a sincere compliment, and he swallowed past the lump in his throat before attempting to reply.

"You did the work. I'm proud of you."

An awkward silence followed, and David used the opportunity to untie the heifer and lead her to one of the empty stalls while Faith took the bucket and placed it on a table near the barn door. When he peeked over the stall, he caught her fretting with her dress and hair like she was trying to make herself presentable, and the sight made him smile.

David latched the gate and walked over to join her. "I finished installing the last of the hardware in the kitchen. Would you like to see it?"

For some strange reason, her attitude changed as soon as he asked. He didn't understand why, but her smile faded and she gave him a half-hearted nod instead of replying. He picked up the bucket of milk and followed her outside, but she kept her gaze locked on the large open field behind the house instead of speaking to him during the short walk.

When they made their way inside to the kitchen, he put the bucket on the dining room table and stood quietly by as she moved from one cabinet to the next, inspecting his work. She made the decision to go with a beige paint color instead of white, and he was glad she did because it gave the whole room a cozy and comfortable feel that was very inviting.

"Everything looks wonderful, David."

Her voice was low and solemn, and his curiously finally got the best of him. "Faith, did I say something wrong? You seem upset."

She turned to look at him, and he didn't know if it was real or simply for his own benefit, but she squared her shoulders and gave him a big smile. "I'm sorry. I guess I'm just tired," she replied. "I really appreciate your hard work over the past couple of weeks. It's beautiful."

She broke their gaze and looked at the cabinets again, and he still wasn't convinced she was telling the truth, but he didn't want to keep prying and risk making her angry. When he started gathering his supplies, she picked up his hammer beside the kitchen sink and placed it inside his toolbox.

"So, I guess you'll be heading back to Franklin soon?"

David shrugged. "I suppose so. Mom keeps hinting that she's ready for me to leave. I've taken care of everything on her to-do list, and I think she misses her peace and quiet."

He chuckled when he said it, but Faith either didn't think it was funny or she didn't hear a word he said, because her expression never changed. Their hands touched as he closed the toolbox, and the warmth of her skin sent an electric jolt to the tips of his toes. She glanced at him for a brief moment before turning and walking over to one of the kitchen drawers, where she removed a thick white envelope.

"Thank you so much for your help, David. I believe this is the amount we agreed on."

She handed him the envelope and stood by silently, as if waiting for him to count the money in front of her, but he put it in his back pocket instead. Honestly, he would have done the job for free if she'd let him. Being able to spend time with her was all the compensation he needed.

"Do you mind if I come by and see you before I leave?" he asked.

He expected her to say no, but he was pleasantly surprised when she said yes. He wanted more than anything to wrap his arms around her and pull her close, but instead he tenderly kissed her cheek. He hoped she might turn her head at the last second so he could kiss her lips, but she never moved a muscle.

Disappointed, David picked up his toolbox and left for home.

* * * *

Faith steered the tractor toward the barn and uttered a plea to the Lord for the ancient machine to make it there. For the past two hours she'd listened to it choke and sputter as she tried to get some work done in the field, and it lasted solely on a wing and a prayer. As she neared the barn, she caught sight of David traveling down the main road in Miss Rosemary's wagon, and she waved as he drew closer. Her heart raced uncontrollably, but it wasn't something she wasn't used to – especially when David was around.

She knew from the gossip filtering through the community that he was leaving for Franklin later that afternoon, and she hoped he was coming by to see her like he said he would. It was a moment she'd been looking forward to and dreading at the same time. She'd barely slept since the day he left after completing his work on the kitchen cabinets. She'd even contemplated finding some other job he could do that might keep him in town just a little while longer.

Faith managed to get the tractor a few feet from the barn before it started sputtering again, and she let out a yelp and covered her eyes when her line of vision was suddenly obscured by sparks shooting from the engine. She parked the tractor and killed the motor, but within a matter of seconds the engine was engulfed in flames.

Faith scrambled off the tractor and raced toward the well just as David came careening into her driveway. He'd barely brought the wagon to a complete stop before he was jumping over the side and rushing to help her. Everything happened so quickly she barely had time to catch her breath, but they were able to douse the fire with three buckets of water from the well before the flames reached the barn.

As Faith watched the last few puffs of smoke billow from the engine, she sat on the ground and pulled her knees toward her chest. She fought it valiantly, but her tears won in the end, and as they streamed down her cheeks she didn't try to stop them. It was all too much to handle, and she was so tired of the constant struggle. Maybe it was time to give up and let one of her brothers take over the farm. They hounded her about it constantly. Maybe this was a sign from God that she was meant to do something else.

David sat down beside her, but he didn't say anything, and for that she was grateful. She didn't want sympathetic words or to be coddled like a child. She wanted to be left alone to cry until she had nothing left. She wanted to drain every last teardrop from her body and soul and just get it over with once and for all.

They sat in silence for a long time, even after Faith stopped crying and settled down. When she glimpsed in his direction, she caught him looking at her with a big smile on his handsome face. He pulled a handkerchief from his pants pocket, and his amused expression never wavered.

"Feel better?" he asked.

If he was trying to annoy her, it was working, and as Faith jerked the handkerchief from his hand, she glared at him spitefully.

"Yes, as a matter of fact. I do feel better. I've seen the light, and I realize now that I'm not meant to do this, so I can finally move on with my life."

David scooted closer to her, and when there was barely an inch remaining between them, she held her breath expectantly.

"And here I was thinking you did this intentionally to try and keep me from leaving," he said, softly.

She knew he was joking, and she tried not to give in to it, but she couldn't help herself. Faith grinned as she playfully nudged his side. "Don't flatter yourself."

Her retort made him laugh out loud, and the deep sound of his laughter was like a healing balm to her rattled nerves.

"Look, I know it probably feels like the end of the world, but I promise it's not," he said. "This tractor is obviously very old, and I think it's served its purpose. Don't you?"

She glanced at the broken-down heap of metal and sighed as she thought back to the many times she'd ridden on the tractor with her grandfather while he worked in the field. He taught her how to drive it when she was thirteen years old, and it held a lot of wonderful memories from her childhood.

"The week before my grandfather passed away, I drove the tractor for him because he was too feeble to do it himself. I worked all day in the field, and I can still remember seeing the big smile on his face as he stood beside the fence and watched. He looked so proud."

David reached over and grabbed her hand, which caught her by surprise, but in a good way. Holding his hand felt like the most natural thing in the world. It felt *right*.

"I know I wasn't fortunate enough to have met him, but I have no doubt he was very proud of you," he replied. "And who knows, we might be able to repair the engine. Don't lose hope just yet."

Faith furrowed a brow. "Don't you mean *I* might be able to fix it? I don't think *we* would be able to accomplish much living in two separate towns."

He didn't answer immediately, but when he brought her hand to his lips and gently kissed her fingers, she felt a glimmer of hope stir deep inside her.

"I've been doing a lot of thinking the past few days, and I feel like this is where I belong. I know how strong-willed you are, and I admire that about you, but I want to be here for you, Faith. I was actually coming here to tell you that."

The small flicker of hope she felt began to diminish. "David, I appreciate you wanting to help, but you don't have to save me. I can manage the farm on my own."

He shook his head. "No, I think you misunderstood what I meant."

Before she could question him further, David leaned in close and pressed his lips to hers. It took only a few seconds, but she felt the impact from it through every nerve in her body. He kissed her again, but this one lasted much longer, and when he released her, she gripped his arm to remain upright.

"I don't want to just help you, Faith. I want us to be *together*. I'll understand if you want to take things slow, but please don't ask me to leave you because I don't think I have the strength to do that."

His voice was low and deep and his breath was hot against her skin. It was an intoxicating sensation that quickened her pulse and made her head swoon, and it was unlike anything she'd ever felt before.

"But what about your job?" she asked. "I would hate to see you give that up."

He smiled as she traced her jawline with his fingertips. "My boss is good friends with the fire captain here in Dayton. I'm sure he would put in a good word for me if I asked."

It took every ounce of strength she had, but Faith pulled away from him so she could focus on him without being distracted by his lips and the heat emanating from his body.

"But you left the faith, David."

He frowned as he sat up straight and looked up at the sky. She hated to bring it up, but if they were going to be together, they had to face the fact that it might not go as smoothly as they hoped.

"I've been thinking a lot about that too. I was young and foolish when I left, but now that I'm older and wiser I realize what I've been missing out on. I didn't think I would ever miss this way of life, but I do. I've felt more grounded and at peace since I've been here than I have in a very long time. I'm hoping the Bishop and elders will agree when I speak to them about it."

It made her heart soar hearing him profess his faith and his desire to return to it, especially since she understood the risk he was taking.

Faith placed her hand against his cheek and when he turned to face her, she pulled him close and pressed her lips firmly against his. It was a bold move, and one she'd never dreamed of taking before, but he seemed pleasantly surprised by the way he deepened their kiss. When they parted, they were both breathless.

"So...do you think I stand a chance with your family, or will your brothers give me the third degree and make me jump through hoops before they let me court you?"

Faith laughed. She hadn't considered what her family might think of their relationship, but she wasn't too concerned about it. If she'd learned anything since inheriting her grandfather's estate, it was that she was capable of making her own decisions and forging her own way in life. If they accepted David into the family, that would be wonderful, but if they refused, she still wouldn't let that deter their plans.

"Oh, I'm certain you can hold your own against my brothers, but I'll put my foot down if they give you any trouble. I know how to handle them."

David grinned as he wrapped his arms around her waist and carefully lowered her to the ground. "I don't doubt that at all."

As he softly kissed her cheeks, her nose, and her closed eyelids, Faith sighed contentedly while enjoying the whisper of his warm breath against her skin. After what felt like an eternity, God was finally bringing together the missing pieces of her life...and she couldn't wait to find out what He had in store for her future.

# ABIGAIL'S DILEMMA

## SAMANTHA COLLIER

Abigail Esh watched as the familiar hills and plains of her small Pennsylvania community fell into view. It had been a long buggy ride; they had been travelling for half a day.

She felt a small stab of excitement, at the thought of finally coming home. She had been staying with some friends of her family, who were English, for the past month. It was all part of her *rumspringa*. She had sampled many things in the big city, including going to art galleries and English restaurants. It had been enjoyable, of course, and she wouldn't change the experience for the world.

But she wanted to return to her community, and start life as a fully committed adult Amish. She was ready.

At last. Her family's farmhouse was in view.

As the buggy pulled up, her eyes took in every detail: the old ramshackle farmhouse, the outbuildings and hen house. Home.

The front door opened, and her mother was down the veranda steps. Her eyes were shining in excitement.

"Abigail! We thought you'd never get here," she remarked.

Abigail stepped down from the buggy, embracing her mother. It felt like she hadn't seen her in years.

"Mammi! It is so good to be home," she said. "Where is everybody?"

Mrs Esh smiled, a bit indulgently. "Daughter of mine, have you forgotten the routine already?" They walked up the steps to the house, arm in arm. "Your father and brothers are in the fields, of course. They will return for lunch, as is always the way. Your sisters are quilting, over at Mrs Troyer's, as they do every Tuesday."

Abigail flung herself onto the living room sofa as soon as they entered. "It was such a long trip, Mammi. I feel black and blue all over."

"How are the Carlisles?" Mrs Esh walked to the kitchen as she spoke, getting the coffee she had just made and two cups.

"Very good." Abigail sat up, rubbing her eyes. "They send their best wishes. It was a bit of a whirlwind, staying with them."

"I could imagine." Mrs Esh poured the coffee. "Come, have your coffee. It will revitalise you."

Abigail did as her mother requested, walking to the table.

Suddenly, she stopped. She could see the figure of a man at the front door – tall, dressed in the traditional Amish clothing. He had taken his hat off.

Who was he? She had never seen him before. And her eyes seemed to be unaccustomed to the Amish dress. She had been so used to seeing English clothes that it stood out to her. Well, she would get used to it, again, of course.

"Mammi." Abigail gestured toward the door. "Someone is here."

Mrs Esh rose, approaching the door. "Oh, it is only Nicholas! He is helping your father and brothers; he has been here about two weeks, from another county." She opened the door. "Nicholas! What can I do for you?"

The young man smiled shyly, looking from Mrs Esh to Abigail. "I am sorry to disturb you, Mrs Esh. Your husband sent me to tell you not to prepare lunch today, as we are planning to work through."

"Work through?" Mrs Esh frowned. "Stay for a moment, Nicholas. I will prepare something quickly for you all to eat, which you can take back with you. You can't all work from dawn to sundown without food in your bellies. Please, come in and sit down while I get something ready."

Nicholas hesitated, then walked through the door.

"Abigail," Mrs Esh said, "Could you please pour Nicholas a coffee, while I get the food ready."

"Of course, Mammi," said Abigail, glancing sideways at the handsome, shy young man. Who was he? Why was he working here?

"I'm Abigail," she said. "Please, sit down."

The young man did as he was told. Abigail poured him a coffee, then sat down beside him.

"How did you come to work with us?" she asked, taking a sip of her own drink.

"I was looking for some short term work," Nicholas replied, blushing slightly. "I am on my *rumspringa*, and wanted to experience life outside my community for a bit. My father knows yours, from many years ago, and got in contact." He paused, staring at her. "I'm sorry, but you are Abigail, who has been on your own *rumspringa*?"

"*Ja*," Abigail agreed. "I have only just returned, after staying with some English friends in the city."

"Did you have a good time?"

"I did," Abigail said. She looked at his hands gripping the coffee cup. Strong, and firm. "But I am happy to be home. The city life is not for me. The Lord has made that very clear."

"I am glad," he said, smiling at her. He had the bluest of eyes, the colour of the sky on a bright summer's day.

Mrs Esh came back in, carrying a paper bag filled with sandwiches. She handed it to Nicholas.

"Please, finish your coffee," she said, as he stood up.

"Thank you Mrs Esh, but I must return to work," he said. "And thank you for the food. I am sure we will all appreciate it."

He smiled at Abigail, ducking his head. Then he left.

Abigail stared after him, sipping her coffee thoughtfully.

What a handsome young man. And such polite manners.

It was good to be home, for a lot of reasons. And it seemed that there was one more good reason, although Abigail hadn't realised when she had walked through the door.

The day was full of surprises.

***

Now that she was home, it seemed like she had never left. It was funny, how life worked in that way.

She had already been home a week, and was back into the old routine. And the most exciting thing of all was that Nicholas, the shy young man who was helping her family with the harvest, had asked her out on a date.

She didn't know where they were going, as she excitedly got herself ready on Saturday night. But she knew that Nicholas would take her somewhere appropriate, as well as fun. They had just clicked, right from the moment that she had laid eyes on him at the front door.

But he was shy. She had found many reasons to go and disturb her family as they worked, sometimes bringing snacks or drinks. Her brothers would grin at her – they knew what she was up to. She didn't usually come to visit them so often. It had worked. Eventually, Nicholas had asked her out.

Now they sat in Stoll's restaurant in town, having just finished a hearty meal and laughing over a coffee.

Abigail had never been able to speak so easily to a boy. It was like they couldn't keep up with everything they wanted to say to each other. She felt a glow within her, as she looked at him.

They were just thinking of leaving when the door to the restaurant opened. Abigail turned to look automatically. Then wished she hadn't.

Oh, no. It was Christian Raber. She swivelled quickly in her seat, staring straight ahead. Her heart had started to thump uncomfortably. Maybe, if she was lucky, he hadn't seen her.

But her luck wasn't in. She heard his footsteps behind, approaching their table.

"Abigail." He wasn't smiling. "I didn't know that you were back in town."

She turned and looked at him, a bit fearfully. "Just a week," she said, quickly.

Nicholas was looking from Abigail to Christian. He seemed perplexed.

"I am Christian Raber," the man said, extending a hand toward Nicholas. "Abigail has lost her manners, it seems."

Nicholas took the man's hand, shaking it. He looked at Abigail. "And I am Nicholas Fisher."

She stood up, quickly. "We were just leaving, Christian," she said, walking toward the door. Nicholas' eyes widened, but he stood up, too, almost forgetting his hat on the table as he followed her. He had to go back to get it.

They exited, into the cold night.

Christian stood for a moment, staring after them.

His eyes were cold.

***

"What was that all about?" Nicholas had to run to catch up to Abigail.

She turned, stopping to catch her breath. "I'm sorry," she said. "I know that I appeared rude. But I didn't want to speak to him. He has this idea that he is in love with me, and I have given him no encouragement. Honestly." She blinked back tears, staring up at him.

"What does he do?" Nicholas was frowning, staring down at her.

"Oh, nothing much," said Abigail. She was appalled to find that her hands were shaking. Stop it, she told herself. "He is always polite. He just doesn't seem to understand that I am not interested."

She paused, shaking her head slightly. "I have told him enough times. But he doesn't seem to understand. When I next see him, at Church or Evening Sing or wherever, he asks me out again, as if he hasn't listened at all."

Nicholas assisted her up into the buggy. "I am sorry, Abigail. It is hard when someone doesn't listen to you."

"*Ja,*" she agreed. She tried to shake the image of Christian, in the restaurant, out of her mind. She was on a date, with Nicholas. Handsome, caring Nicholas.

"Don't worry about it," she said. "I am sure he will realise, eventually."

They rode off, into the night.

They didn't look back. If they had, they might have seen the figure of Christian, standing in the dark street, staring after the buggy long after it had disappeared.

***

"He was in Stoll's Restaurant, Mamm."

Abigail was having a hot cocoa with her mother after the date. Nicholas had dropped her off half an hour ago.

Mrs Esh frowned. "Don't read anything into it, Abigail," she said. "It might have been just co-incidence. Who knows, maybe he needed to get something from Stoll's."

"At nine-thirty on a Saturday night?" Abigail was frowning, too. "No, I know him of old. He followed me there, I am sure of it."

"He never threatens you, does he?" Her mother looked at her over the brim of the mug.

"No." Abigail shook her head. "He is always polite. It's just a feeling I get. He always seems to be where I go, and he won't stop asking me to date him. I think after the first three negatives, he might get the message that I am simply not interested in him in that way. But he never does."

Mrs Esh stood up. "Time for bed, I think. I will talk to your father about this. We don't want to offend the Raber's, but Christian needs to know that he can't harass you. We will have to think it through carefully, though."

Abigail nodded, bringing her mug to the kitchen sink.

"I almost forgot." Her mother looked at her. "How was the date with Nicholas? We got so caught up talking about Christian."

Abigail smiled broadly. "It was lovely," she beamed. "I think that I really like him, Mamm. Do you think he likes me, too?"

Mrs Esh smiled, her eyes softening as she looked at her lovely daughter. "How could he not, my *lieb*?" she replied. "But I don't know how long he is staying for, Abigail. Your father said that he only needed help for a few weeks, and they are almost up. He lives in the next county."

"That's not so far," said Abigail. "We could write letters."

"So you could," agreed her mother. "But it really is time for bed now, Abigail. We have Church tomorrow, don't forget. And I have to be up very early to cook the goose for the lunch."

Abigail followed her mother up the stairs, preparing for bed. She glanced down at her Bible, thinking whether she should look at it tonight or not. It was very late. But she was still feeling jittery after her encounter with Christian, and felt like she needed some comfort.

Her head was drooping over the good book when she suddenly jolted fully awake. What had disturbed her?

She took her candle, and got out of the bed, walking to her window. She peered out into the darkness, but she could see nothing. She tried to shake the feeling of unease away from her. She was being silly. She should blow out the candle, and climb back into bed.

And yet she stayed, staring out the window. It was complete darkness; not even the moon was out tonight, and a thick blanket of clouds had covered up the stars.

She dropped the curtain, and climbed back into bed.

But the unease didn't leave her. Instead, it invaded her dreams...

*She was running.*

*In motion, she suddenly stopped. She looked down at her feet, willing them to move. But it was like they were frozen in quicksand; the more she tried to dislodge them, the firmer they set. She twisted and turned, in a frantic bid to free herself.*

*He was coming. She knew he was right behind her.*

*Suddenly, the quicksand turned to ice. She attempted to run, again. But her feet were sliding over the ice. She stumbled, trying to regain her balance.*

*She heard a noise behind her, and turned quickly.*

*It was him. She couldn't see him in the shadows, but she knew.*

*The ice started cracking underneath her feet. She watched it zig-zag, broken veins across the white surface.*

*And then she was gone, underneath the ice, plunged into cold, cold water.*

*She stared up, and saw him looking down at her, coldly...*

She sat up in bed, breathing heavily. She could feel sweat sliding down her neck.

This had to stop. She didn't know what Christian's intentions were, but he had to know how much he was scaring her. She didn't think that he would harm her, not really. But he was behaving oddly, and she couldn't deny anymore that it was starting to affect her.

She lay back down, drifting back to sleep. Think happy thoughts, she told herself.

The image of Nicholas filled her mind. His handsome face, concerned for her that night when she had told him about Christian. The way that he had helped her down from the buggy when they had arrived home, holding her hand tenderly so that she wouldn't slip. She had looked into his eyes, and seen kindness. His eyes shone with the purity of his soul.

Nicholas. Was she falling in love with him? But she hardly knew him. It had only been their first date, and they had chatted a handful of times before.

And soon he would leave. Return to his farm in the next county, away from her. His *rumspringa* over, just like hers was.

Would she see him again?

The image of Nicholas was the last thing that she remembered as sleep finally claimed her – this time for the whole night.

***

Abigail yawned, trying to stifle it with her hand discreetly.

It was the next day, and she was tired. It had been late before she had finally drifted off to sleep. She looked around at the familiar faces at the church service, but she hadn't seen him yet.

Nicholas. Her heart leapt as she said his name in her head, over and over.

Where could he be?

She tried to concentrate on the service, but her mind was drifting. Her mother had told her that Nicholas had attended their church service since he had been staying with them. And he himself had said that he would see her there. He had been looking forward to her mother's baked goose with apple and cider gravy for lunch, as well.

She surreptitiously scanned the congregation, again. But then she saw Christian Raber, staring at her from the back row. Shivers coursed through her; her skin crawled like it had been invaded by an army of ants.

She looked to the front, trying to concentrate on the service.

But her eyes, sickeningly, were drawn back to him.

He hadn't stopped staring. But now he added a small smile.

She refused to smile back. It would just encourage him. Silly, she chided herself. Even turning her head to look at him again he would perceive as encouragement.

He had always been an intense boy, ever since they had shared a seat in the one room classroom down the road. She could remember that he often would be alone, kicking a stone in the playground while groups around him played. And when he had friends, it would always be only one person, or two. Usually children who were a bit odd, like himself.

She had never been anything but polite to him, but she had drawn the line at friendship. She just couldn't stomach his intense stares. How he had perceived her politeness as anything other than that was beyond her. And yet he had. He had been asking her out for over six months now.

At first, she had been flattered, despite herself. But then it had got annoying. He simply wouldn't listen to her, when she said no. And then he started turning up everywhere that she went: a visit to the bakery, or when she was perusing stalls at the market. Anywhere.

It was one of the reasons she had gone so far away for *rumspringa*. Abigail wasn't much of a traveller, really. She probably would have stayed closer to home. But she had needed a break from his constant attention.

The service finally finished, and people started socialising. She went up to her mother.

"Where is Nicholas?" she whispered. "I haven't seen him today."

Mrs Esh looked at her. "I'm sorry, I forgot to tell you, Abigail," she said. "Nicholas received a note this morning, about something urgent. He needed to return home immediately. I'm not sure if he will be back, my *lieb*. He was due to finish work soon with us, anyway." She looked at her daughter. "Cheer up! You can still write to each other."

Abigail felt her heart sink. She shouldn't be so disappointed, of course. They had only had one date, and Nicholas had a life of his own, far away.

But she *was* disappointed. She couldn't deny it.

She was staring at the wall of the barn, lost in her own thoughts. She didn't see Christian approach until it was too late.

"Abigail." He bowed, slightly. His cold eyes were assessing her, as always. She often felt he looked at her like something strange he had just discovered on the sole of his shoe.

"Christian, I'm sorry, but now is not a good time," she said, quickly. Why was he always silent when he approached her? If she had some warning, she could have scurried away.

"I hear that the young man you went on a date with last night has left us," he continued, as if she hadn't spoken at all. "Very suddenly. Did you know that Frannie Glick knows him and his family? She was just telling me that he has a fiancée, back home."

Abigail gasped. She shook her head. "No, Christian, I am sure that you are mistaken," she replied. "Nicholas didn't mention anything to me about a fiancée. He is an honourable man."

"Is he?" Christian smiled, coldly. "How well do you really know him, Abigail?"

She frowned. She supposed it was true, to a degree. She had only known Nicholas a week, after all.

But she trusted her instincts. He was a good man, she knew it. He wouldn't have deliberately deceived her about having a fiancée.

"Well, I shall talk to him," she said, turning away. "I really must go, Christian. I have to help my mother with the lunch."

She walked away quickly, ducking amongst people. Hopefully he wouldn't follow her.

Was it true? He had said he had got the information from Frannie Glick. She looked around, but couldn't see her.

She frowned. Oh, well. Frannie would turn up, sooner or later. And then she would ask her, how she had come by this information that Nicholas had a fiancée.

As Christian claimed.

She felt the skin crawling on the back of her neck. She looked around, and, of course, he was staring at her. An upsurge of anger shot through her. Would he ever leave her alone?

***

"He did mention a girl he had been dating..." Mrs Esh frowned, squinting her eyes, trying to remember. "Or was it that they had dated in the past? I'm sorry, Abigail. I simply don't remember. But he never mentioned a fiancée, of that I am sure."

Abigail frowned, too. It wasn't the simple yes or no answer that she was wanting. This was very frustrating.

She didn't have a right to demand an answer of Nicholas. They had made no promises to each other; it had only been one date, after all. But she also felt that he did owe her an answer, because it simply wasn't done to be dating someone behind his fiancée's back, if he had one.

If it was true, she never would have agreed to go out with him. It was as simple as that.

Restless, Abigail stood up. "Do you need me for anything else, Mamm? If not, I might go to my room, study my bible for a while."

Mrs Esh looked at her. "Of course, Abigail," she said. "Just come down to help with supper, that's all I require."

Abigail left, bounding up the stairs.

Mrs Esh watched her go, shaking her head slightly.

Her daughter was in a state, and had been since Nicholas had left so suddenly the day before. Mrs Esh was worried about her. It was unlike Abigail. And what was this business with Christian Raber? Abigail hadn't mentioned it to her until after her date with Nicholas. If it was true, it wasn't good, and they should intervene on her behalf. But what if Abigail was just being fanciful? The Rabers were good friends of theirs. Mrs Esh didn't want to cause conflict without reason.

She frowned, pondering. No, they would do nothing, for now. If Abigail continued to be worried, well, they would do something then.

She sighed. It was hard, being young. Navigating your way into adulthood. She might mention some bible passages that Abigail should study, to try to ease her mind.

***

Abigail finished the letter, signing her name at the bottom thoughtfully.

She had been in two minds about whether to write to Nicholas, but she was so wound up she didn't know what else to do. Even if she didn't send the letter, it had felt good to get her thoughts and feelings out onto paper.

She read back over what she had written. She had tried to not be too intense, but still convey her wish to continue corresponding with him. She hadn't mentioned anything about him having a fiancée, except to implicitly imply that if he was seeing someone where he lived, she would stop communicating with him.

She put the letter in an envelope, and sealed it. She wasn't sure of his address; she would have to ask her mother if she knew it.

She left it on her desk, propped up against her lantern.

It was time to help her mother with supper.

*** 

Outside the farmhouse, Christian could see Abigail leave her desk. He saw the letter. He could guess who it was to. And he knew how to solve this, as well.

He often watched her. He had found a position, quite hidden. He would come over the back way to the house, through the fields, being careful to avoid her father and her brothers working.

He didn't think that he was doing anything wrong. He had, after all, explained to her that he wanted to take her out. It was his intention to make her his wife. She was hesitant, and had said no, but that didn't unduly concern him. His father had told him that girls sometimes said no when they meant yes. His own mother, apparently, had refused his father a few times before finally agreeing to date him.

She just needed a little bit of persuasion, that was all.

He frowned, thinking of when he had walked into the restaurant and seen her on a date. It simply would not do. No other man was allowed to date his Abigail.

It had been a stroke of luck that Nicholas Fisher's father had suddenly needed him back at home; as soon as he had heard that, he seized the opportunity. Frannie Glick was away on her *rumspringa*, and couldn't contradict his story about a fiancée. Frannie was a friend of his, anyway, and as soon as she was back he would contact her and persuade her to corroborate the story.

He smiled. It was all going to plan. He had to get rid of Nicholas once and for all, discredit him in Abigail's eyes. And then he would be there, to pick up the pieces.

She would finally see that he was the one for her.

***

The letter had been sent. Abigail waited for a response, but none came.

Inside, she fretted a little. It was all so strange. She had thought that she and Nicholas had a real connection. But he wasn't responding to her – did that mean that what Christian said was true? That Nicholas had a fiancée back home, and that she had been a diversion while he was away?

But as the days went by, and no letter came, Abigail had to admit it to herself. Nicholas didn't care.

Oh, well. She went about her chores as normal, and smiled and laughed when she was required to. She let no one see her sorrow. It would get better, in time. Of course, it would. They had only known each other a short time. It wasn't as if it was a deep wound.

She studied her bible. The classic passage from Ecclesiastes 3:4, about there being a time for sorrow as well as joy, comforted her. She knew that life couldn't be good, all the time. You could learn from sorrow, and had to accept that sometimes there was sorrow in life. As surely as the tides ebb and flow on the shore, sorrow and joy would come and go.

So Abigail kept telling herself, as the days drifted into weeks.

***

The women sat around the table, picking up their needles to commence their quilting bee.

Abigail picked up hers with a sigh. It had been three weeks, and she had not received a word from Nicholas. It was time to let it go, put it behind her. They had connected, but he had decided that it wasn't worth pursuing. Or, he did have a fiancée at home, and he had been merely dallying with her. Abigail preferred to think it was the former; she didn't want her last impression to be that he was a dishonourable man.

They heard another buggy pulling up outside the farmhouse. The women looked at each other.

"Are we expecting someone else?" Mrs Esh turned to the women.

Frannie Glick walked through the door, puffing slightly.

"Frannie!" Mrs Mueller put down her needle. "We weren't expecting you! Aren't you supposed to be on your *rumspringa*?"

"*Ja*," answered Frannie, smiling at the group. "I returned yesterday, a few days early. Mammi told me that you were meeting today, and I wanted to catch up with you all."

Frannie took her seat, and started answering questions about her *rumspringa*. She had been staying with cousins in Ohio, and had a wonderful time.

Abigail glanced at her as she worked. She was waiting for the break, so she could ask her about Nicholas. It probably didn't matter, anymore. But she wanted to know.

At last, the women started getting up. One went to the kitchen, to prepare coffee and snacks. Frannie rose, and walked to the window.

"Frannie," Abigail said, walking up to her. "It is nice to have you back. I was just interested to know. Christian Raber was telling me that you know Nicholas Fisher and his family."

"Who?" Frannie looked at her, a puzzled expression on her face. "I don't know any Nicholas Fisher, Abigail. I think you must be mistaken."

"Are you sure?" Abigail frowned. "Christian told me that you knew the family, and that Nicholas had a fiancée back where he lives."

Frannie continued to look at her, bewildered. "I have no idea what you are talking about, Abigail. The only Nicholas I know is Nicholas King, who we went to school with."

"I'm sorry," Abigail said. "I must have misheard him. Thank you, anyway."

She turned around, and walked out of the house. She needed to be alone, for a moment. She needed to think.

She sat down on a seat on the porch, thinking deeply.

Frannie didn't know the Fishers. She had never heard of Nicholas. Which meant one thing: Christian had lied to her. About Frannie knowing them, but also about Nicholas having a fiancée.

She felt herself go cold. This was getting serious.

Christian had always been an annoyance. But now, he was actively interfering in her life.

She didn't know what to do. Just that it had to stop, once and for all. He had no right, and she was going to make sure that he knew it.

****

Abigail dressed carefully for the meeting.

She had spoken to Mrs Raber, asking her could she come over for a visit. There was something she needed to discuss with her and her husband, urgently. She also requested that Christian be there for the meeting.

She didn't tell her mother. She knew that she would be concerned about making waves with the Rabers. It was something she was concerned about, too. But she also knew that it couldn't continue. Christian had to be stopped. And the best way of ensuring that was to enlist his parents. Abigail knew Christian. He was obedient to his parents, and his father ruled him with an iron fist.

And it was something that she felt must do, by herself. She had to stand up for herself, once and for all.

Mrs Raber opened the door, and led her to the kitchen table. Coffee and cakes were there, waiting.

"Oh, you shouldn't have gone to so much trouble," Abigail said. She was sweating, a little, and her hands when she took the coffee cup were shaking. She wasn't looking forward to this.

Mr Raber was already there, looking at her expectantly. And then Christian came into the room.

He didn't look happy. But he sat down at the table. Obviously, his parents had insisted.

"So." Mrs Raber looked at Abigail, expectantly. "What did you need to see us about so urgently, Abigail?"

Abigail cleared her throat. She must be strong, but she was very nervous. It could backfire on her, and the Rabers might evict her from their home, saying that she was lying.

How should she proceed?

"Thank you for seeing me," she stated. "I know you are all busy people. I needed to see you about Christian."

Christian looked at her, his face like thunder. She almost balked, but doggedly continued.

"As you know, Christian and I have known each other a long time," she said. "Since school. I have always liked him as a friend, but lately, Christian has been wanting to court me."

Mr Raber smiled. "Nothing wrong with that."

"No," Abigail continued. "There isn't. But I have told Christian many times that I am not interested in him that way, and he continues to pester me. He doesn't listen to my wishes."

Mrs Raber looked at Christian, anxiously. "Is this true, Christian? Have you been pestering Abigail, when she has clearly said no?"

"She wants to go out with me," Christian blurted. "I know she does! She just needs persuading. Isn't that so, Daed? You always told me that women often don't know their own minds, and need a firm hand."

Mr Raber frowned. "That is not what I meant, Christian. Yes, sometimes a girl takes a bit of wooing. But if a young woman has clearly said no to you, repeatedly, then you must do the honourable thing and accept her decision."

"But...but..." Christian shook his head, colouring. "I know that she loves me, deep down!"

Abigail looked at him, coldly. "That is wrong, Christian," she said. "I don't love you, and never will. I have no desire to hurt you, but you must accept what I say. I don't want to court you. I like you just as a friend." That was a little white lie. She didn't like Christian, at all. But she didn't want to completely destroy his confidence in himself.

"Abigail, your wishes will be respected," said Mr Raber, glaring at his son. "I will make sure of it. Christian will not bother you anymore."

"Thank you," breathed Abigail. She turned to Christian.

"I wish you well, Christian," she said. "I hope that you find the woman that you will marry, one who loves you. But she is not me. I hope we can still be friends. Will you shake my hand?"

She offered her hand across the table to him. He looked at it as if he might refuse, then he grudgingly shook it. Mrs Raber looked relieved.

"I must go," said Abigail, rising. "Thank you all so much for letting me speak, and taking me seriously. It means the world to me."

"God speed, Abigail," Mrs Raber replied. Mr Raber smiled at her.

It was over. Christian would not bother her, again. She knew the Rabers, and that they demanded complete obedience. Christian would not dare to defy them, now that they knew. She would have preferred that he realised by himself, but that might never happen.

She had to protect her life. He had already interfered in her budding relationship with Nicholas. She didn't want him to interfere for a minute longer.

***

Abigail was feeding the hens when a shadow fell across her.

Fear gripped her. Oh, no. It wasn't Christian back – was it?

She looked around. Then gasped. It wasn't Christian who stood there, but another tall man.

It was Nicholas!

She stood up, slowly. She couldn't quite believe that he was here.

He smiled at her, a bit tentatively. "Abigail," he said. "Your mother said that you would be here."

"Here I am," she replied, then could have kicked herself. Couldn't she think of anything better to say?

"Do you want to go inside?" He asked. "I need to talk to you."

She nodded, leading the way out of the hen house.

They sat at the kitchen table, staring awkwardly at each other.

"I thought..."

"I'm sorry..."

They laughed, as they realised they had both spoken at the same time.

"You go," said Nicholas, looking at her as if he had never seen her before in his life. It made her glow.

"I thought that you didn't want to see me again," Abigail said, biting her lip.

"I thought the same," Nicholas replied. "When you didn't answer my letter."

"What letter?" Abigail frowned. "I never received a letter from you. I wrote *you* a letter, which you never replied to!"

Nicholas shook his head, frowning. "I don't understand. I never received a letter from you. But I did send one."

Abigail stared at him, perplexed. Then understanding started to dawn on her face.

"It must have been Christian," she said. "I didn't realise he was going to that level. He must have been monitoring our mail box. Mamm leaves letters we want to send in there for Daed to collect and send when he gets to town."

"Christian?" Nicholas frowned. "That man who has been pestering you?" He paled, and stood up. "This is going too far. I will go around to his house, this minute!"

"Nicholas, sit down," Abigail said. "It's alright. I have spoken to his parents. He won't be bothering me anymore."

"Are you sure?" Nicholas sat down, slowly. "Because if he ever tries again, he will have me to answer to!" Abigail could see a vein throbbing in his temple. He was angry.

"So you care about me?" She looked at him, shyly.

"I do," he replied. "So much so, Abigail, that I travelled here today to speak to you, even though I thought you didn't answer my letter." He paused, looking like he didn't know what to say further.

"I care for you, too, Nicholas," she said, shyly. "Can we begin again? Like before Christian started interfering in our lives. He told me you had a fiancée, back home."

"He what?" Nicholas looked gobsmacked. "That is an outright lie! I would never have asked you out on a date if I had a fiancée. You didn't believe it, did you?"

"I tried not to," Abigail answered. "But when you didn't reply to my letter, I thought the worst. It was Christian, all along."

"We can begin again," Nicholas said, looking at her earnestly. "If you are willing?" He reached for her hand, across the table. "And God willing, of course."

"Nothing would please me more," Abigail replied. She took his hand. Happiness swelled up within her.

Christian was out of their lives. Nicholas cared for her.

The time for joy was upon them.

THE END

# SADIE'S AMISH PURPOSE

## MEGHAN MASON

Faith came through the labor of her first child a little worse for wear. It had been twenty-three agonizingly long hours of pain and worry. The good part was that she and her husband, Luke, were now blessed with a new boppli boy. After the birthing process, Faith had been far too exhausted to even hold the poor little boppli, let alone choose a name for him. Luke tried as best he could to manage the boppli alone. The midwife had mentioned that a case of the baby blues was a normal happenstance of childbirth, what with all the tumultuous hormones and all, but Luke was quickly feeling overwhelmed with trying to care for an infant, plus keep an eye on Faith as she tried to recover. It was getting a bit too much to manage. Luckily, Faith had a cousin, Sadie, who was a little older than the average Amish woman, and was available to help as a nurse to the child and to Faith, so Luke felt that now was the perfect time to broach the topic with Faith,

"Dearest, I know you have not been feeling yourself these past weeks, and I think it would be wise to ask for some help with the boppli?"

Faith, being still moody after the birth, turned her head, tears streaming down her face, as his words had unintentionally reinforced her own sense of inadequacy,

"Sure, Luke, if that's what you think is best," she cried. Luke felt terrible over causing more tears, but this was just the situation that was continuing to be a challenge,

"Oh no, Faith! No tears! You are doing just wonderful. Maddie, the midwife, said that this was a perfectly normal reaction to the hormonal fluctuations in your body. Many women go through this after the birth of a boppli. Do not feel badly over it for a second. I was thinking it would be a nice change if we asked your sweet cousin, Sadie, to help with the household chores. You can oversee boppli, and designate any other chores to Sadie," he answered, trying his best to make it sound as positive as possible. He watched closely as Faith rolled back towards him, trying her best to force a smile,

"Ok, my dear Luke. I understand it has been hard for you to handle everything on your own. Let's write to Sadie at once, then," and Luke handed her paper and pencil.

Faith had written Sadie a letter, trying not to sound overly desperate, but Sadie could tell that the new father was ready to return to the fields, and she could sense that her cousin was feeling a little depressed. Sadie had heard tale of women feeling moody after the birth of a child, although she could scarcely understand why. It was her dream to have a child, but as the time flew by, her chances of marrying and becoming a mother grew slimmer by the minute. This was of no consequence, as she knew how much Faith needed her. She put aside all other responsibilities to care for Faith and the boppli. There was not a job in the world that sounded more exciting to her in that moment than caring for her cousin and little one.

She currently lived on the outskirts of Wilkes County, so the letter had arrived with some speed. This proved lucky for Luke, who was at the end of his rope, having been dealing with soiled diapers, helping with all the laundry, and trying his best to serve as family cook. That turned out to be somewhat of a disaster, since all he did was either burn everything or serve it all miserably undercooked. He was all for being a new parent, but Amish men belonged in the fields, doing manual work for the family, whereas a woman's place was homemaking and child rearing. He hoped his wife would feel better soon, so that their lives could return to normal. Little did Luke understand that with a new boppli, there was never to be the same sense of normalcy.

Sadie had received the letter with an open and willing heart, as she had nothing much else to keep her busy nowadays. She was now well past the marriageable age of most Amish girls, being thirty already, and having had no offers of marriage, nor any suitors over the years. It had been a hard pill to swallow, being the only girl to be passed over in the entirety of Wilkes County. She had not been an unattractive young girl, but she was plainer than the rest of the girls her age. This had led to many lonely evenings at home with her parents, and since her teens and early twenties, all her bruders and schwesters had gotten married and left home. She had been left to care for her parents, but they had started their family very young, and were not nearly so old as would need constant care from their daughter.

Sadie recognized the opportunity to help her cousin, Faith, for what it was. It would be a life of servitude, although not forced, because she loved Faith, and she loved taking care of wee bopplis too. However, it was still a lonely life once the family no longer needed her help. Perhaps Faith would keep her on as a helper if she had additional bopplis. That is what Sadie wished for at the very least. Plus, Luke was a nice and upright man, who treated Faith with more respect than she had ever witnessed. Most Amish men were quite honorable, but Sadie had seen a few friends and one schwester end up with a domineering husband. Lucky Faith had been blessed two-fold with a proper husband and a beautiful little boppli. She considered the whole plan sheer providence, and packed her bags with delight, thinking of all the good times ahead with her cousin's family.

By the next morning, Sadie was safely in her father's buggy headed towards the other end of the county. There was so much to think about, as she gazed at the lovely fall foliage. October was her favorite time of year,

"Oh, daed, look at all the changing leaves!" she cried, "they are so many rich colors of gold, orange, yellow, and just a few green leaves still peeking through. By November, there'll be almost no leaves at all. Snowfall brings its own magical beauty, but I prefer the change between summer and fall. It's like a kaleidoscope of color!"

Her daed glanced up at the trees as he held the reigns,

"True," he declared, "there is no prettier time of year than fall, in my humble opinion, Sadie. But more important than the changing leaves is your new job of helping your cousin Faith. She's going to be needing lots of tender loving care, as your mamm put it to me last evening." Sadie understood what he was hinting at, since Gracie, her eldest schwester had given birth six months ago now, "When Gracie had baby Fern, she struggled with the moods for some many weeks."

"I know, and remember it well, daed," answered Sadie. "In fact, I consider it a good thing that I had a trial run of it with Gracie. Now I'll know what to expect with Faith. I do feel sorry for her, this being her first boppli and all. She should be enjoying this special time instead of feeling out of sorts. Funny how some women get moody and others don't..." and she trailed off as the gorgeous surroundings of the woods captivated her imagination. She imagined a walk through the fallen leaves, running, and then jumping into a nice big pile of leaves. Then again, she was much too old for that frivolity now. She was a grown-up woman, but without the glory of having her own family, she thought sadly. How thrilling it would be to play with her own children and her true love amongst the golden fall beauty.

Time passed rather quickly, and it was not long before Sadie and her daed pulled up the drive to Luke and Faith's farm. Luke was just coming out the front door with a basket to fetch eggs when they arrived,

"Well! If it isn't cousin Sadie and Uncle Fredrick! Welcome, and come right in," and he helped Uncle Fredrick tether the horses. Sadie grabbed her two small bags, and in they went to have tea and cake with Luke, Faith, and the new boppli,

"Isn't he just the cutest ever?" squealed Sadie, and she gathered up the boy and snuggled him, smelling the top of his little newborn head. There was nothing like the scent of a newborn, she thought, as she tucked the little one back in his cradle.

She glanced around the kitchen for Faith, but found no one there except an apron covered in flour and egg shells. Then she noticed poor Luke's plaid shirt, all dirty with the fixings of making a carrot cake! Faith must be worse off than Gracie had been. At least Grace had been able to move about the house, and do minimal choring. It looked as though Luke was primarily on his own with everything around the house and baby too! She was going to have her hands full with running around the house, plus looking after baby and mother too,

"Luke, if I may be so bold as to inquire, how is cousin Faith coping?"

"Ah, no good, I'm afraid," he said, "she goes from feeling alright to weeping for no apparent reason."

"Well, have you had the doctor in for a look at her?" she asked.

"Yep, Doc Spencer says she'll be right as rain come a few more weeks, but it's been hard taking care of boppli. He doesn't even have a name yet! Every time I ask Faith what we should call him, she starts to crying. I don't know what I'm doing wrong," Luke said with exasperation.

"I'll see what might be bothering her, but somethings just take a little healing time, Luke. It's nothing to worry yourself over unless it gets out of hand. I'm here now, and all will be well soon enough. Tomorrow morning you can start about your outside choring, and I'll do my part inside with Faith and this little one, "and she gestured towards the cooing boppli in the cradle. Luke seemed glad to hear all of this, and headed off to bed early that night to get plenty of much needed rest. As for Faith, Sadie prepared her a bowl of stew she had prepared once daed had gone, and made up a cheery tray. There was a bowl of hearty beef stew, cornbread, and a glass of milk. Sadie dropped one of the last flowers of the season into a bud vase, and carried it into Faith,

"Hello, cousin. How are you feeling?"

"I'm not too well, Sadie," she said slightly above a whisper. "I don't want to burden Luke anymore with these blues I've been feeling, and I'm afraid I haven't been very much help."

"Never you mind that right now," said Sadie, and she urged her cousin to eat.

After the bowl was clean, and the cornbread left only half eaten, Sadie figured she'd better ask Faith about what she wanted to call the boppli. He could not be nameless any longer, and that was the first hurdle topping her list of challenges,

"Faith, now Luke has been fretting over what to call the boppli. Do you have a favorite name in mind?" She could see Faith's face darken a bit, but she confided in Sadie instead of her usual crying spell, which as actually a positive step in the right direction,

"Sadie, was Gracie this way too?" she wondered. "I feel so all alone, and there are no other women in the village that have gone through these baby blues."

"Yes, it's strictly temporary, but we've got work to do if you want to be up and around in the next few months. Lying here day after day isn't doing you any favors. That's how we got Gracie to snap out of it. Now, let's start with naming boppli."

"Alright, if you say so," and she looked sincerely relieved to hear this news coming from a woman instead of Doc Spencer. It was easy to talk to Sadie. They had always been so close as young girls, but since she had married Luke, her girlhood relationships had taken a backseat to her husband and their growing family. "How about Isaac? That was Luke's daed's name, so I think that would make Luke feel happy."

"Sounds like an excellent choice to me!" exclaimed Sadie, and the two shared a few giggles, and played with Isaac, which was a vast improvement for her cousin. The next month proceeded much the same way, and it was not long before Sadie's infectious kind ways and loving heart were becoming a part of the new household.

Faith eventually found her way back to normalcy, thanks to Sadie's constant support and Luke's unwavering love. By two months, Faith was fully capable of caring for Isaac full time. She still needed some assistance with chores, so it was agreed that Sadie would stay on for an indefinite amount of time. Sadie loved the idea, because she had the joy of proximity to Isaac, and Faith and Luke were quickly becoming an important part of her life. She cooked excellently, and her meals were even becoming sort of legendary within the small village. It was a perfect fit for all concerned.

Just a few days later, Faith returned from a walk to town with baby Isaac in the pram. They had gone to mail a few letters, and she had returned to the farm brimming with news of everything that was happening in town,

"Sadie! I'm home," and she searched out her cousin in the chicken coop gathering fresh eggs and tending to the new chicks. "You'll never guess what's been going on! Old farmer Gregor finally passed away, which of course is sad news, but the exciting part is that his nephew Abraham has reportedly inherited his land. He's due to arrive in two weeks, and a committee of ladies is being formed as a welcome group. I volunteered you! You're to be his cook and housekeeper for the first month of his stay. By then he'll be sure t find a wife, and you can return to life here with us," and Faith and Sadie walked back to the kitchen to feed Isaac his afternoon snack.

"I wish you would have consulted me first, Faith. It's not a problem for me to do this service for Abraham, but I am sure a younger lady would have been much more appropriate if he is looking for a wife. He must be nervous coming to a new county and inheriting a new farm. I'll hardly be very thrilling company for the poor man," lamented Sadie.

"Nonsense!" cried her cousin, for Faith knew that Abraham was a bit older than the average young farmer, and Sadie was still pretty, even though she qualified as an old maid at thirty years old. Faith believed that this would be an advantageous situation, given that it was rumored that Abraham was not handy in the kitchen, and needed a housekeeper too. These were natural talents that Sadie had been blessed with, and she was caring too, which would serve him well being new in a strange village. At the very least, Sadie would make a new friend, and Faith would have a little more room to get used to doing more household chores.

Late that following Friday afternoon, Abraham ambled into town on his horse, carrying what little belongings he had in his buggy. The committee was there to welcome him to Wilkes County, and introduce him to various members of the town. Faith and Luke, being pillars of faith in their community, explained to Abraham all he needed to know about worship, work, and social life. They explained to him that there was to be a social after worship in two weeks' time, and that everyone looked forward to meeting him. He got settled at Old Farmer Gregor's property, and Sadie was sent to prepare dinner and keep house. She was to make the moderately long walk from Luke and Faith's farm to the next farm, which was now Abraham's.

As Sadie stood at the counter slicing vegetables, Abraham engaged her in conversation,

"So, Sadie, is it?"

"Yes, my name is Sadie. What can I do for you? I'm in the middle of cooking your supper, so it'll have to be quick," she replied, trying not to sound annoyed that her cooking was being disturbed.

"Oh, in that case, I'll wait to talk. It smells heavenly, whatever it is," answered a confident Abraham.

He was a handsome man, sure to be a big hit with the young ladies who were vying for a husband, she thought, and she continued to prepare the roasted chicken with care. She wanted to please him as a cook, so that she might stay at this post for as long as possible. She had grown used to the community, and did not relish the dismal thought of returning to her parents on the other end of the county. There was absolutely nothing waiting for her there, and at least here, people appreciated her for what she could offer; excellent cooking, strong faith, and limitless kindness for others. This was not going unnoticed by Abraham, to which Sadie was oblivious. He was about thirty she guessed, but it was usual for a man like him to take a young wife, and be ready to start a family and tend to a farm or similar livelihood.

When the chicken was roasted to perfection, and the vegetables and potatoes were finished boiling, she laid out a place for him at his table. She called him to supper time, but once he saw only the one place setting, he insisted that she join him,

"Heavens, no! There is so much great food here for only me. Surely you can sit and join me. If I may now regale you with some light conversation," he joked, since she had put him in his place earlier. Though unorthodox for the two to sit together, she agreed. He seemed congenial and honest, and she was truthfully quite hungry,

"So, tell me, Sadie, what brings you here to my farmhouse to help with choring?"

"I have been elected to serve as your housekeeper and cook until you find a proper replacement," she replied matter-of-factly.

"Oh, you mean until I am suitable married to one of the eligible young ladies?" he smiled.

"Well, yes, that's the way things normally go. You know that," and she did not appreciate him playing as though he did not understand what was expected of them all.

"And, you, Sadie, what is expected of you?"

"Nothing," she stopped short, and did not know exactly how to reply to this, as she was never asked before.

"May I ask why you are not amongst the clamoring ladies looking for a husband?"

She shied away, and stared at the floor, not knowing if he meant to be insulting or what his purpose was. He had to know that at her age she was considered a spinster, though relatively the same age as he was. That was tradition, and as Amish, they all knew full well what was expected. She continued to look away, feeling ashamed and saddened that she had not been chosen to be a wife and mother. It was enough to bear the brunt of the feeling of failure every day, but she was wholly unused to being confronted with the obvious truth of her situation.

Abraham seemed to notice her discomfort, and immediately regretted his comment,

"Please, Sadie, I apologize if I have made you feel less than what you deserve," and at that she looked up in some surprise. What she *deserved*? Wasn't this what she deserved? She was bound to a life of serving others through faith, perseverance, and volunteering in the community to help those in need. That was what she thought she deserved, and nothing more. She had resigned herself to her fate, and did not appreciate the fact thrown in her face. She felt embarrassed and self-conscious, but stood up for herself nonetheless,

"I beg your pardon, Bruder Abraham, but I am too old for marriage, and you, being an Amish man should know this. I have been elected to serve you because I am not what one would consider eligible, and no one need fear for my reputation at my age."

"That, Sadie is one of the most stupid things I have ever heard, and yes, I know full well what is traditional for Amish, but that does not mean I have to agree with it. What is wrong with you? Nothing! You and I are probably the same age, and you are attractive," at which she blushed furiously. No matter how hard she tried, she felt the heat in her cheeks increase, although she felt a twinge of instant attraction for a man who spoke his mind, and who also thought her pretty. What would she say to a man such as this, she pondered, but she blurted out what came into her head,

"Why! Bruder Abraham, while I thank you for the compliment, I think it better that you concentrate on your chicken. There is blackberry pie for dessert, but none for you should your dinner be left unfinished," and they sat in relative silence for the remainder of the meal, though Abraham felt vindicated with the offer of freshly baked pie!

Their banter continued as such during every meal, becoming more and more relaxed with one another, though Sadie knew her place. She was perhaps a friend, and nothing more. She would not fool herself into believing anything more. Besides, Bruder Abraham had been away for three out of five dinners this week alone. Parents were inviting him to meet daughters, and he was being plied with all the best traditional foods the women of the house could manage. As if a streusel would entice a man to marry, she clucked, as she finished the dishes from the day, and prepared to sit down with a nice, hot cup of mint tea. She was determined to enjoy her times alone, and either read a book or sit with a cup of tea until Abraham arrived back for his late night habitual coffee. She did not understand the man's need for coffee that late at night, but her job was not to question why, but only to fulfil her duties to the man. She was growing fond of spending time with him, and even enjoyed their lively conversations about social conventions and everyday talk of farming, food, and faith. They never ran out of topics to speak about, and he insisted she join him for every meal.

Just as she retired to the couch for her tea, she heard Abraham and his buggy in the yard. Home early tonight, she thought, and went to put the kettle back on the stove for coffee, "And why are you home so early this night?" she inquired.

"Ah, no reason besides a little boredom," and he hung his hat on the stand, and plopped down on a chair, "Would there be any corn fritters left over from last evening?"

"Why would you want fritters when you just came from supper at the Smith farm?"

"Because the women are apparently not very good at cooking! They may have beautiful and upright daughters, but your corn fritters are by far the best in all the county, Sadie," he said with a hint of a smile, though he looked exhausted of going out almost every night to meet new families and their daughters. Sadie had a few fritters left, and warmed them at the stove. She served them with his coffee, and sat down to her tea across the room.

Abraham devoured a fritter and a gulp of coffee, and then launched into conversation,

"Sadie, enough is enough. You know we get along well, and I have already said that I find you attractive. Why must I continue going to these ridiculous suppers, when I know what I want out of life already?" Sadie rocked in her rocking chair, completely oblivious to what was about to be said between them. She felt they were friends and good ones at that, but nothing more.

"Sadie, are you listening to me?" he said, as she stared off into her book, "I am trying to speak with you, and you've got your head stuck in a book?"

"I apologize, Abraham, what on earth do you want to talk about? Aren't you too tired for anymore frivolous conversation after all these suppers?"

"That's exactly the point. Why should I go elsewhere when I am happy here at home?" he asked, as she just sat there, mouth agape, and provided the expected answer,

"You will not be allowed your bachelorhood for very much longer. You may as well choose one of the many pretty girls, and put an end to this coming and going..." she sighed. She knew in her deepest heart of hearts that she loved Abraham, but that destiny was not hers, and she had accepted that fact very early on. She looked up from her bible readings, and found Abraham looking at her differently than most nights,

"I am done with the suppers. You are right, Sadie. They will never give up until I have chosen a wife. In fact, that is one reason why I am home early tonight, besides the terrible cooking," he jested. She put her tea down upon the table, and she felt the sadness she expected to feel once he had made the inevitable choice. No matter her own feelings, she knew what was coming next. He had found one of the Smith girls acceptable, and this was what he was trying to tell her, that he would not much longer be in need of a housekeeper or a cook. Abraham continued to look at her, so she figured she'd better say some congratulatory words, even if she feared her displacement was imminent. Not only would she lose her new friend, but she would have to return to her parents in the east of the county,

"What can I say, Abraham? This is wonderful news that you have chosen a wife for yourself. I will miss keeping house for you, but now you must make room for a wife. No doubt there will be many preparations to be made for a wedding," and she went back to reading her verses.

"Yes, no doubt about all that fuss, though I am a simple man. And, yes, I have decided on a wife. But I hope you'll stay on to cook and clean for me after I am married," he said straight faced.

"You of all people know that is impossible. If you didn't enjoy her cooking, you had better choose someone else then. No wife is going to want an old maid hanging around the house," she countered.

"No, I don't suppose she would, but sometimes old maids make the best wives," he said, "so in theory, I would not have to let you go, nor would I have to choose a better cook." He looked at her expectantly, though he knew well enough that he was treading on thin ice with her. He thought for certain that they would make the perfect pair, despite the unwanted gossip from the townspeople.

"I do not appreciate your jokes, Abraham. Make a choice, and do not mock those of us who have a different calling in life. Being an 'old maid' as you so nicely put it, has its advantages," though she couldn't really think of a good example just then.

"Woman, are you really that dense that you do not understand my meaning? I am saying in the best way possible that I prefer my wife to be the old maid that I already love!" She looked at him utterly astounded. If this was not the cruelest joke ever played, she did not know what could be worse. However, Abraham looked at her sincerely, and looked expectantly for some sort of answer, so she replied,

"Ha ha, Abraham. You've had your little joke at my expense. Now off to bed with you, and after that stunt you can bet there won't be any more extra fritters!"

"No, no, dear Sadie! I am saying quite deliberately that you are the wife I have chosen if you will have me as your husband. We make a good match, you and me. We are the same age, we love the same things, and we are excellent friends. Why not that I should choose you? You are the best choice for me, and that is the way I want our lives to be. Not this stiff situation of living as acquaintances, when we both know we are suited well for one another. Please say yes, Sadie, or make me a miserable old Amish man who never marries or has any offspring!" he declared with so much vigor that Sadie had little other choice but to believe him.

"What? Me? I am just that, an old maid. Besides, I may not be able to bear children..." and he stopped her there,

"That's nonsense. Women your age bear children all the time. The only difference is that they are already married by this time. Stop devaluing yourself! I love you, Sadie, and you're not going anywhere unless you say you do not love me too. Now what do you say to that?"

She stood now, tea cup clattered to the floor, open-mouthed in total surprise, but she already knew what her answer was to be,

"Yes, I do love you," she blushed, "and I do want to marry you too, but you will set the tongues a-wagging by choosing me over the younger ones!"

"I do not care about wagging tongues. I care about keeping the woman I love in my home, and making her my wife."

"Then yes! I do accept." She bent down to pick up the pieces of shattered cup, but Abraham beat her to it, and began to gather the pieces. "I guess we will need a new set of cups for our first wedding gift," he said seriously, but the humor was not lost on Sadie. She let out a giggle, sounding more like a school girl than a grown woman of thirty. Her parents and Faith and Luke would never believe this turn of events in a million years, though she was utterly happy to accept the proposal. Not only was she to be married, she was to marry a man who she felt real friendship for, and sometimes that was a rarity in marriages.

# Four Months Later

The wedding was very simple, and her parents came in the buggy, and Faith, Luke and Isaac were the only guests in attendance. Not by circumstance, but by choice. The simpler the better, they both thought, and they had already sent the town into a flurry of confusion as to why Abraham would choose a spinster as a wife, but he had quickly put them all in their places, quoting Jeremiah, 29:11,

"For I know the plans I have for you," declares the LORD, "plans to prosper you and not to harm you, plans to give you hope and a future."

Once Abraham's words had been passed around town, there was no one who could argue otherwise that the marriage should take place. So, a hasty date was set, allowing for travel time for Sadie's thrilled parents. They initially did not know quite what to make of the situation, but after meeting Abraham, they were relieved to know that he was an upstanding Amish man, who loved their daughter very much. Her daed even lamented losing a great cook to Abraham, to which her mamm had good naturedly bristled, but all knew that Abraham was to become a very fortunate man.

Eighteen short months later, Faith announced a second pregnancy, but the true celebration was about to begin, as Sadie confided in her cousin that she too was expecting a child. It was more than she could have ever dreamt of! God had blessed them all beyond measure, and now the cousins would be having their bopplis very close together. The second cousins would grow up being the best of friends!

# 9 months Later

Sadie had felt that nine months was hardly enough time to prepare for the arrival of a new boppli, and she had worked tirelessly knitting and crocheting baby things. She and Faith even joined a quilting circle and made two new little quilts for the upcoming new additions. They both chose yellow and green fabrics, not knowing ahead of time whether they would be blessed with boys or girls. Sadie secretly wished for a baby girl, so that she could make her lots of dollies and play clothes, while Faith had been hoping for another little boy. Luke prided himself on his son, and was praying for a big group of bruders for little Isaac, but Faith had put her foot down at having two. Luke was to be happy with whatever he got, and he loved to joke relentlessly that Faith would be a new mother again and again, delivering son after son to a proud and overjoyed father. Whatever the case was to be, Luke reminded Faith what a time they had had with baby Isaac, and that a healthy, bouncing boppli was all that he truly cared about.

Labor pains began for the two women almost a day apart, and a brand new, precious boppli girl was born to Abraham and Sadie, and they named her Esther, because Abraham had had a spinster aunt that had died childless and alone. Esther was a tribute to her, and to the blessing that had been bestowed upon them. However, before Doc Spencer and the midwife could gather their things, it was obvious that Sadie was still in distress of labor pains. The only conclusion to be made, was that another sweet boppli was about to make an appearance!

"Twins!" Abraham exclaimed upon hearing the news from the birthing room. He was overjoyed, though Sadie was shocked to say the least. Here she had thought it would be difficult to have just one boppli, but here they were with two. So, Esther had a sister, and her name was to be Ella. Ella had long been a favorite name of Sadie's since her childhood, so it was only fitting that one parent named one daughter, and the other named the second little dear one. Esther and Ella would be the happiest set of sisters the village had ever seen.

As for Faith and Luke, they had another boy, and called him Abram, not to be confused with Abraham!

Sadie's mamm and daed decided to move closer, so her mamm could help with all three bopplis. And so it was that the blessing was four-fold, three new bopplis, and grandparents close to boot. God had been good to all of them, and much joy was to be had by all involved. Even the townsfolk did their best to help with the extra work of three bopplis in two families.

Abraham had never been prouder of any decision that he had ever made before in his life. Marrying Sadie had been the best thing ever, and now their little family was complete.

Little did Abraham and Sadie realize then, that two more bopplis would make an appearance in the coming years. Their happy family of three would turn into a family of five, with two little bruders for the girls. They were born one year apart, and Sadie's heart was filled to brimming with gifts she never thought would be hers.

# THE BIG AMISH ADVENTURE
## ERICA FANNING

It was a beautiful, sunny day in the little community where Joshua Miller lived, and he was excited about this particular day. He was taking his little sister, Miriam, to her first Rumspringa event. Since Joshua was the eldest son of the Miller family, he had the pleasure of taking the younger siblings to their different functions in the family buggy. From where the Miller's lived the church was on the other side of the community, which happened to have a 2-lane highway that went through for the Englishers that lived in the two neighboring towns on either side. Joshua's parents had learned to trust him because he had been able to successfully avoid an accident with cars on more than one occasion, but they seemed to be unsure now because Miriam would be with him.

"It's not you that we don't trust," Mrs. Miller tried to explain. "It's those cars... they're always driving like it's the end of the world. And even after the state changed the speed limit through the community, they still don't really slow down. Please be careful."

"We love you son," Mr. Miller added. "We just want to make sure you and Miriam get back safely and in one piece."

"Don't you worry," Joshua said, confident in his maneuvering abilities. "I will make sure that Miriam and I come back to you the way we left." He smiled reassuringly, which seemed to settle his parents some.

The trek to the church was extremely uneventful. Even Miriam commented that it seemed quiet for a Sunday afternoon.

*Maybe going home will be just as easy,* Joshua thought to himself. *Especially since it will be later in the evening.*

What nobody counted on was someone asking Miriam on her first night to court him, or at least Joshua didn't count on that. Samuel Stoltzfus was a nice young man that the Miller family had seen a lot of growing up because he had always been interested in Miriam, but somehow it slipped Joshua's mind that he would be there. For Joshua, it was just another night to fellowship with his friends; he wasn't interested in a lot of the young women that were interested in him, and the ones that he would have been interested in were taken already.

"Looks like you'll be going home alone again, Joshua," Samuel poked him as he walked past, leading Miriam to his buggy. Joshua simply smirked and shook his head. He enjoyed not playing the courting game that everyone else seemed to be playing. He wanted to take it slow and let his life play out as smoothly as possible. These days, that included not worrying about another person in his life.

On the way home, Joshua began mapping out the next day in his head. It was a great way to pass the time and that's all that he really had as he guided the trusty steed along the side of the road. As usual, there still weren't many cars around, but a lot of them seemed to be driving dangerously close to Joshua. Secretly, he was glad Miriam went home with Samuel; he hoped they got home safely.

And then it happened. Before he even had a moment to process what was happening, he was thrown from his seat. A sharp pain bit into his leg and he yelled in pain. His head hit a rock and the last thing he remembered someone was emerging from a dark muscle car asking him if he was okay.

He knew he wasn't. *This is the end of life as I know it.*

He awoke slowly. Everything around him seemed white and clean. He had never seen any Plain dwelling like this before.

*Where am I?*

A woman moved into his vision. Joshua attempted to move his head and thought better of it when a thousand pins and needles shot down his spine. He winced from the pain and something to his right started screaming. The woman—who was wearing dark blue scrubs—quickly moved toward the noise and fiddled with something before the sound stopped and Joshua began to feel better. He opened his mouth to speak, but all that came out was a cough.

"Hello there! How is my favorite patient doing?" The nurse seemed to be yelling at him, as if she thought he was deaf.

"Water," Joshua managed to croak out.

"Sure thing!" The volume hadn't gone down; maybe that's just the way she spoke, he decided.

After he had a few sips and felt he could form a coherent sentence, he asked her where he was.

"Well," the blonde-haired woman began. "You're in the hospital. You've been here for about a week. After your family released you to our care, we had to do some emergency surgery…"

Joshua was confused. "Emergency surgery? On what?" He checked all appendages; hands, arms, legs, feet… Something felt off. His left leg moved just fine, but he couldn't get his right leg to cooperate. After some repositioning, he looked down. Where his right leg should have been, there was simply… nothing.

"I'm so sorry," the nurse said, but Joshua didn't really hear her.

"What happened to my leg? What did you do?" He felt panicked. What was this? All of the pain he felt when he first woke up was suddenly gone as adrenaline took over. "Where is my leg? What did you do?!" Red began to creep into the edges of his vision as loud beeping came from his right. A few large men in white and two more nurses rushed into the room and began holding him down.

"Sir, please calm down." Everyone spoke calmly but firmly, though Joshua didn't hear it.

"How can I live like this? How will I live?"

Panic was the last thing he remembered before sleep overtook his mind completely.

It took a full week of waking up in a panic and having to be sedated before Joshua woke up one day and finally seemed to grasp what had happened. He had lost his leg due to an infection from an accident with a reckless driver and now there was no real future for him in his community.

*People won't accept me,* he thought bitterly. *I've seen how they treat outsiders. I've seen how they treat the sick. They don't care about them and just want to pretend they don't exist.*

No matter what his family tried to tell him over the next few weeks, he decided he was going to get his own little abode in the community and live on his own. Joshua's father had been looking into it with him before the accident. While Joshua had been in and out of consciousness in the hospital, Mr. Miller and Joshua's younger brother, James had completed it to fit Joshua's new life. Joshua didn't like the way that sounded and instantly decided no matter how nice it was he wasn't going to like it.

A Mennonite friend of Mr. Miller's, Mr. Benjamin, took them from the hospital on the day of Joshua's release to Joshua's new home on the edge of the little community. Since Joshua had such a low expectation of his new home, nothing he saw surprised him or changed his mind. For his father and younger brother, he put on a smile and told them how much he loved it even though he wanted to raze the small dwelling with everything in him. He hopped out of the van with the help of his mother and the hospital-issued crutches.

*There is no way my life could be any more humiliating right now,* he thought to himself bitterly. *My mother is helping me out of a Mennonite's van, coming from an English hospital because I have only one leg. There is no way I could be more humiliated.*

He was quickly proven wrong as the entire community came to his new home to welcome him back. He knew it was all fake; there was no way he was going to let these people into his life when they didn't want anything to do with him before. He played along for the time. He didn't want to disappoint his mother, who was more than overjoyed at the outpouring of "love" the community was showing not only Joshua, but his entire family. Miriam was already shown a lot of attention because of her blooming relationship with young Samuel Stoltzfus, but Joshua noticed how much the other members—both young and old—showed her more respect. At that moment, Joshua decided he would go along with the love and care he received if that meant his family was shown the same love and care. They deserved it. They worked hard for it.

Joshua just wanted to be left alone. That's all he ever wanted, but for his family he would be the most outgoing person the community had ever known.

A few weeks later, during one of the required physical therapy visits, John, the therapist brought up an interesting proposition to Joshua.

"Mr. Miller," Joshua hated that the young man called him that, but allowed it when it seemed like he really had something on his mind. "I don't normally bring this kind of stuff up... but you don't seem very happy." Joshua sighed. This was one of the rare days that only Joshua was home while John was there.

"You know what, Johnny? I'm not." Joshua decided to just be honest. "I no longer have a leg, I have a community who pretends to love me and a family that doesn't know what to do with me. They gave me this house even after everything because they thought it was best to move on, but really all it does is make me feel farther than ever from them. Because now they have to come to me, and that requires them being on the same road that I was on when my accident happened. I just wish that none of this had ever happened."

John stopped what he was doing and looked Joshua in the eyes. "I can't bring your leg back, but I can do the next best thing. What do you think about this new prosthetic that a doctor friend of mine has been working on? It would almost be like you never even lost your leg."

"Does it take the phantom pain away? Because if not, you can't even make that claim."

"Well," John had a small gleam in his eye. "From the few people I've heard that have used it... yeah." That stopped Joshua.

"Really?" John nodded.

"Obviously, giving you a limb isn't going to fix your relationships, but it will help you get out of the house and start to take your life back. That's a good start, don't you think?"

That question almost seemed rhetorical, so Joshua didn't bother to answer. John went back to helping Joshua with his exercises and the day went along without another incident or mention of this possible new freedom.

For the next two weeks every time John was there—whether someone was there with Joshua or not—Joshua asked about this new prosthetic. Everyday, the pros seemed to outweigh the cons more and more. One day, Mr. Miller confronted Joshua about it after John left.

"Son, do you really want to do this?"

"Dad," Joshua figured there was a lot he was doing that his father didn't know about. He wasn't about to keep calling him Father as if he really honored him. "At this point, I'm practically an invalid. People are always coming over and giving me food as if I can't cook. They bring me blankets as if I don't have a whole extra bedroom full already. I don't need people's sympathy! What I need is to get my life back!"

Joshua didn't realize he was yelling until he really saw the look on his father's face. It was full of shock and hurt. Joshua thought for sure his father would remind him to respect his elders, that he would give him the what-for, that there would be a yelling match. What his father did scared him more than anything that had happened in Joshua's life until this point.

His father simply nodded once, gathered his coat and hat from the rack, and turned back to his son for what would be the last time he would probably ever set foot in Joshua's home again.

"Just know that whatever happens, I will always love you."

With that, Joshua's father was gone. When the door closed behind him, Joshua felt seriously alone for the first time in his life.

Amanda Waller was a petite, young blonde woman straight out of nursing school. She began working for Dr. Jacob Zimmerman, the doctor who had developed the smart prosthetics, the very next day. For her, it was a dream come true. Not only did she have one of the best-paying jobs in the city, but she also got to work with the man she had considered a father figure in her life.

As Amanda was restocking some of the completed prosthetics in the supplies closet, John came in. Although Amanda was not registered as a physical therapist, she had learned a lot from John in the two short months she had worked alongside him. It helped that John had a brand new Amish patient that he could use as an example without having to worry about too many details being spilled to the wrong people. Since Amish people don't have friends outside of their own communities, they never knew what was or wasn't said about them. However, John was very honorable and would never divulge more than was necessary for a good, short lesson in P.T.

"Hi John," Amanda called. She heard John sigh and looked back to see him sitting in a chair with his head in his hands. She immediately left her stocking duties and moved toward him. "What's wrong?"

He looked up at her and shook his head. "I don't understand why I agreed to help an Amish person. They hold themselves back for a religion? A belief? What? I don't understand. And I have the unfortunate privilege of trying to convince this man if he really needs a prosthetic. He's unhappy, Amanda. I want to help him."

"Well if he's unhappy, that's not something you can fix." If anybody knew that, it was Amanda. She had tried to find solace in drugs, alcohol, and sex before fully giving her life to God. She may not have agreed with everything the Amish people did, but she knew there were good people in Amish communities who really loved God. "Sometimes the ones that need help the most are the ones who don't want it."

"But that's the thing," John retorted as Amanda found a chair and sat down next to him. "It's not that he doesn't want it; his family doesn't want him to have it." Amanda shrugged.

"Okay, then he doesn't get it, right?"

"Amanda, he's 20. He is legally old enough to make his own decisions." Amanda had seen photographs of the man, Joshua Miller. He certainly looked like he could pass as 16 on any given day.

"I have an idea," Amanda was about to tread into some unfamiliar waters. "What if maybe he just needs someone different to push him and his family over the edge? If this is something that will at least help him, maybe they just need a different way of looking at things." John looked at her questioningly.

"Are you sure? I mean, I don't want you to get into trouble. And you're not registered as a physical therapist."

"Maybe not, but I have a great teacher." She smiled at him before adding, "Besides, we can consider this a trial run for some field experience. There's only so many supply closets I can stock before we run out of space." They both chuckled.

"I've never really seen Dr. Zimmerman say no to you," John stated after a moment. "I guess we can at least run it by him."

Joshua just wanted to get rid of the pain. He had no family, no friends, no livelihood... and no leg. What else was he to do? His parents would be ashamed if they knew what he did with his days.

*There's no way I can tell them what's really going on. There's no hope for me.*

The only thing that kept Joshua going was his weekly visits with John and the possibility that he could turn his life around with a prosthetic. He finally decided that the next time John came, he would say yes to this new prosthetic.

There was a knock at the door. Joshua grabbed his crutches and hobbled over. When he opened the door he saw a petite blonde-haired woman, not much taller than five feet with a cute bob, standing before him.

"Hi Joshua," the woman said as if she were a messenger from Gott and knew all of his dirty little secrets. "My name is Amanda, and I will be your new physical therapist. May I come in?"

Joshua had never let a woman into his house without another person that he knew already there. Of course, Joshua was living a life of firsts, why would he stop now. Amanda began shifting her weight between her feet, probably trying to figure out what he was thinking. He finally opened the door and moved out of the way.

"Looks like you're moving well with the crutches," she seemed to be making small talk, but as soon as Joshua closed the door Amanda got right to it. "Okay look, I know you didn't want a female here because you didn't want the people of your community to think weird things were going on here, but hear me out." She paused to take a breath. "John told me he had been having some trouble convincing you and your family that the prosthetic was the way to go. I offered to come to help you ease your mind. See, I work with the prosthetics all the time. I'm not an actual physical therapist, you might say... really I just stock the closets and make sure the patients do well after the integration surgery but—"

"Get to the point." Joshua had had enough of the rambling. Amanda looked at him strangely for a minute, and then nodded.

"The point. Well, the point is, I want to help you and your family put your minds at ease about this decision to use this new prosthetic."

"I don't have a family."

"What?" Amanda looked confused by that statement.

"I don't need family to live. It's just me now. And I've already made up my mind that I want this prosthetic."

"Oh," she looked a little crestfallen. She had prepared a big speech and defense and it appeared as though she over-prepared. "But, just for the record, you do still have family right? They're not... dead or something?"

"To you, they might as well be." With that, Joshua hobbled toward the kitchen, effectively ending any form of conversation about his family. The last thing he wanted to talk about was what gave him so much pain. He took a couple glasses and a bottle of amber liquid and poured two small portions in each cup. He handed one of them to Amanda.

"What is this?"

"Scotch."

"Are we celebrating something?"

"The fact that my life is about to change." Joshua tilted his head and drank his portion in one swig. Amanda simply stared at hers as if she was debating.

"I'm sorry," she finally handed her glass back to Joshua. "I'm on the job." She smiled as if hoping that would ease the rejection of the drink. What she didn't realize is that Joshua intentionally poured her portion so that he could drink it when she refused. He had yet to see a nurse or physical therapist, or whatever they called themselves, drink any kind of alcohol unless it was purely by accident or they were tricked. Joshua didn't understand why you would want to trick someone into drinking alcohol—people either like it or they don't—but he had heard a lot of stories during his stay at the hospital.

Joshua finished her drink in one swig before setting the glasses down and asking her what he needed to do. It seemed as though Amanda was sent to convince and not necessarily to prepare for integration, so although she had little concerning her function this time, she promised the next time would be different.

In three days, someone would pick him up and take him to the clinic where he would be put under for surgery. There were pieces that had to be tapped into his spinal cord and nervous system so it was just like any other limb. As Joshua listened to Amanda talk, he knew he had made the right choice.

*Maybe I can convince my parents of that when they see me with my new leg,* he thought. He could only hope.

Amanda felt a little defeated leaving Joshua Miller's home. Something seemed off the entire time and she wasn't able to put her finger on it. The man seemed cordial enough for someone who was still dealing with the loss of his leg, but there was something else about him that seemed to make Amanda edgy.

*Well, I have a while to figure it out,* she thought to herself. *I'm stuck as his P.T. now, thanks to John and Dr. Zimmerman.*

The conversation only a few days prior had gone better than expected. Dr. Zimmerman had been debating throwing her into the field for some practice and figured who better to send his beloved Amanda to than a nice Amish family. What no one realized at the time was that this Amish family was falling apart at the seams and not even a limb could save it. So much could happen in the week of a patient of this caliber, and Amanda knew that, but something seemed different about this family. About Joshua.

Three days later, a few men came and picked Joshua up in a van much like Mr. Benjamin's and took him to the clinic for preparations. When they arrived, both Amanda and John were standing there waiting for him.

"Hello Joshua," John said as he opened the door. "It's good to see you here! Are you excited?"

Joshua simply nodded. There was no more need for words. Of course, it didn't help that everything seemed louder and brighter. Talking seemed to be difficult these days when that happened. Amanda noticed the flash of pain in his eyes and was more gentle with her tone and volume.

"Hi Joshua," she almost seemed to whisper, but that's all Joshua needed. She looked him in the eye and for the first time Joshua really noticed how blue her eyes were. They were a striking contrast to the deep brown of John's, who also had blond hair. If Joshua didn't know better, he would have thought they might be siblings.

As the van drove off, the trio walked into the clinic together. Amanda helped Joshua fill out the necessary paperwork while John went to the operating room to prepare with Dr. Zimmerman.

"How long will this take?" Joshua was sure Amanda had told him already, but he was so nervous he couldn't really function. She simply smiled understandingly and went through all of the information she had just gone through. Just as Joshua began to relax, John came to them and said they were ready. By then, he was ready as well.

**Two months later**

Joshua wasn't sure how Amanda kept managing to come back everyday when he would treat her like trash everyday. He just couldn't really function...

Amanda knew Joshua had been drinking. The only reason she kept coming back and didn't request that John take his patient back was because she knew that Joshua was better than that. She had seen him after the surgery. He was a completely different man. He was kind, funny, smart, and he knew how to hold a conversation.

Since coming home, Joshua went right back to his old habits. Amanda kept waiting for the right time to bring it up, but that next day might be the one. Joshua threatened her for the third time in as many days; he was getting worse. Every time he said something to her, it irritated her in some way. Did she have feelings for this broken Amish man who hadn't had contact with his family in almost four months?

The answer was a resounding yes. Because not only was he broken, he was attractive. Although he hadn't worked outside in almost six months, he still had a nice tan and chiseled skin with which his dark hair and soft, brown eyes flowed nicely. Amanda might have thought he was Native American if he hadn't told her some of his story about his family and growing up in the community. Something about this Amish "bad boy" really threw Amanda into a bind. John noticed it one day when she returned to the clinic one day.

"Aw, you have feelings for him," then he lowered his voice. "You have to be careful with that though. He is a patient. If you want to keep him as one, you need to make sure your feelings stay out of it."

Amanda already knew all of this, but it was good to have the reminder.

Joshua didn't understand Amanda. She was enigmatic as she was beautiful. He could tell that she knew about the drinking, but she hadn't said anything to him. Was she supportive of it? Did she hate it? Why was she being so silent about it all the time?

Joshua decided the next time he saw her, he would confront her. He wanted them to be totally open with each other.

The next day, when Amanda came to help Joshua with another rough day with the new prosthetic, he asked her the hard question.

"If you know about my drinking, why haven't you said anything to me?"

She was quiet for a few minutes as she avoided the question and focused instead on the physical therapy part of it. Regardless of what happened, in just under a week, Joshua would be done with physical therapy and they would never see each other again. He wasn't afraid to ask the question because he knew he would never see her again.

"Because I love you," she finally admitted. Joshua was taken aback. "I thought they were just feelings, but I realize now that I love you. I didn't say anything because I was trying to find the right words to say. You might think I have a way with words, but I really don't. Most conversations I start, I thought up on the way here from my house everyday. I can't imagine life without you, Joshua Miller. Even if I had to leave my dream job behind... I would do that for you." It was quiet between them for a few moments before Joshua spoke.

"I don't deserve your love."

"Is anyone deserving of the love they receive from another person? We learn how to love from the One Who created us, from God Himself. He loved without hardly ever receiving anything in return. No one who is loved ever deserves it. But that doesn't mean that we don't still give it. Joshua, you're still not talking to your family and it's been months. In fact, I don't even know what your family looks like if I needed to. For you to have no relationship with anyone in your family isn't right. You pushed them away, but for what? For alcohol? Because they upset you? Because you feel like you failed? Well guess what? Don't you think they feel like they failed? You were alone when you were in your accident! One of the biggest jobs for a parent is to keep their child safe. There is no greater failure for a parent than when they have to see their child get hurt and then reject all love from them."

By the time either of them realized Amanda was on a roll, it was too late to stop.

"You might think you're protecting people by keeping them out of your life, but really all you're doing is hurting yourself. Please Joshua..." she moved closer to him, inches away from his face. "Stop pushing me away." Without thinking about it, Joshua grabbed her face and pulled her in for a kiss. He had never kissed a woman before, but something about the way he did it and the feelings he got from it seemed right. Just like with the prosthetic, he knew Amanda was right. Not only in what she said, but in who she was and what she meant to him. He pulled her away to look into her eyes. There were tears in them.

"That was great... but do you really love me, Joshua?" She whispered so quietly, he almost missed what she said, but when he caught it his heart broke into a million pieces and he crumpled to the floor and wept. Amanda kneeled next to him and they just held each other and cried for a long while.

Joshua let it all out. All of the pain, the hurt, the feelings of anger toward the community, the feelings of betrayal against his family. He asked Amanda to pray with him to God to ask for forgiveness for everything that he had done and said. When they were finished, he felt really clean for the first time in a long time.

"There's still a few other things you need to fix before you can move on with your life... but we don't have to worry about that today." Amanda stood to leave.

"Wait!" Joshua was surprised at his sudden urgency. He pulled himself up so that they were standing toe to toe once again. "I want to fix that today."

Amanda looked at him for a moment. "Are you sure? That's going to be a hard wound to heal."

"Then it's the one I need to work on," Joshua said resolutely.

"Okay," Amanda grabbed her keys. "I don't care what you want to do, we're taking my car to get there." He smiled.

"I can agree to that."

Ten minutes later, Joshua and Amanda pulled up to Joshua's parents' house. Miriam and Samuel were on the front porch talking. When Miriam saw Joshua she jumped up and ran inside, leaving Samuel alone and confused.

"Hi there," Amanda called. Samuel simply waved, so Joshua made introductions. As soon as he finished, Miriam burst out of the house with the rest of the Miller clan on her heels. They all rushed Joshua so quickly that Amanda had to move out of the way to avoid being trampled. She moved to stand by Samuel while there was much crying from the family.

"How do you know the Miller's?" Amanda asked Samuel.

"I'm courting Miriam," he answered simply. "We're getting married in the spring."

"Congratulations," she smiled, then turned her attention back to the Miller's. After a few more minutes of hugs and tears, Joshua finally broke free.

"Mother, Father... I need to tell you something," he began. Mr. Miller put his hand on his eldest son's shoulder.

"No you don't, son. All you needed to say, anything you've done... it's been forgiven. It's done." His father smiled at him, and Joshua knew in that instant that anything he wanted to say didn't need to be said. But he had to do it for his sake.

"Well then let me tell you anyway. I went with the prosthetic and it's finally working like it's supposed to, thanks to Amanda." Joshua pointed to where she was standing as she waved awkwardly. He held her gaze for an extra moment before looking back at his parents. "But I gave into the sin of alcoholism. I pushed everyone away because I didn't want you all to see me as the failure that I am."

"Honey, we have *never* seen you as a failure," Mrs. Miller interjected. "We're just glad to have our son back." Joshua smiled, and Amanda realized he wasn't done.

"There's something else... this bit of news is a little harder to give." Joshua rubbed the back of his neck awkwardly. "I want to leave the Plain lifestyle." Miriam and James gasped, Samuel's eyes went wide, but Mr. and Mrs. Miller simply looked at each other and nodded.

Mrs. Miller explained, "When we saw you pull up with Amanda, we thought you had already."

"I don't think I could have left without saying goodbye to the people that brought me into this world and taught me everything I know about how to be a man of God." Tears filled Joshua's eyes again and he almost cursed because he promised himself he wouldn't cry. "I love Amanda, and she's shown me so much about how to live life. She's shown me a new perspective every time she's talked to me... and really she's the reason I'm even alive right now." He looked back at her and she had a mixed look of shock and love on her face. Joshua chuckled inwardly. "I know this seems like a bad time to be leaving right after making amends but—"

He was cut off from his mother crushing him into a hug.

"You just go and be the man you know God is calling you to be," she said as she pulled away.

"Wait," it was Amanda. "You—you're leaving now?" Joshua seemed confused by what was happening.

"Yes. The sooner, the better, right?" Amanda came down from the porch.

"No, not right. Joshua, your sister is getting married in the spring! If you excommunicate yourself now, you'll never be able to see her get married! No! You need to stay. At least until your sister gets married. But only if I get an invite." She had said that last sentence directly to Miriam who, until that point seemed the most devastated by her brother leaving. All you could see on her face in that moment was a smile.

"Anything to keep my brother here for a little while longer," Miriam sighed, relieved that he would be around to help with preparations.

"Besides," Amanda added. "It gives Joshua time to test out how well his leg would work in a Plain lifestyle." She looked at him and winked.

Over the next few months, Joshua and Amanda spent as much time as they could repairing relationships with the community and getting to know each other as individuals instead of as therapist and patient. John was less than excited about the sudden change in Joshua and Amanda's relationship, but Amanda realized it wasn't as sudden as she thought.

Once someone's true feelings are out in the open, everything happens very quickly. It's the journey to that point that seems the longest and the hardest... but it is the best journey because that is where true love is born.

**Springtime, Miriam's wedding**

Joshua was glad he waited until after the winter season to leave. Spring was always his favorite season growing up, and now it seemed like he was seeing all of the colors for the first time. With Amanda's help, Joshua had gotten off of all alcohol. He had repaired all relationships with the community and was even loved by all. He realized he had been too hard on them all in the beginning. It's not that they faked the love they had, it was that they didn't know how to show true love.

The preacher had asked Joshua if he wanted to take over the community's preacher position when he retired, but Joshua had made up his mind that he was leaving with Amanda the day after his sister's wedding.

"It's so beautiful," Amanda whispered beside him, just low enough that only he could hear it.

"Yes, you are," he whispered back. She gave him a scolding look as the preacher finished the vows with Samuel and Miriam.

"You may now kiss the bride."

Cheers and applause came from the open air as people stood from their seats to welcome the new union of Mr. and Mrs. Samuel Stoltzfus. Joshua was glad Amanda made him stay; he wasn't sure he ever would have forgiven himself if he left too early. If there was anyone he was going to miss, it was going to be Miriam.

In the receiving line, Joshua hugged Miriam extra tightly and whispered in her ear, "I love you Miriam. Be good for me. Write often." When they pulled back, there were tears in both of their eyes. They laughed.

"Ah, don't be such a softy," Miriam joked, before wiping her eyes and turning serious. "I love you, brother. You be good as well. It's a big world out there." He nodded.

"But I have a great woman and an even bigger God that will help me navigate." They both smiled.

"How did it go?" Amanda asked as they walked to her car. Joshua was quiet for a moment.

"Well."

"That's it? You're leaving your family forever and all you have to say about the last conversation with your sister is that it went 'well'?" Joshua laughed.

"No, but I need to process it before I can just go around telling people what happened. Let's move on to the next big adventure of our lives."

"You mean the first big adventure."

"For you maybe." They looked at each other for a minute before Amanda turned over the engine and drove away toward the city, leaving everything Joshua knew behind him.

*I never thought my life would go this way, but I can't imagine it ending any other way.*

*For that, Joshua was glad. He didn't like having all of the answers anyway.*

9 798224 597543